Dual Visions

By
Herbert Grosshans

Published by
Melange Books, LLC
White Bear Lake, MN 55110
www.melange-books.com

ISBN **978-1-61235-014-1**

Credits

Editor: Jane Carver
Copy Editor: Taylor Evans
Format Editor: Mae Powers
Cover Layout: A. Bratt

Dual Visions
by
Herbert Grosshans

The Cliffs of Time

Dinosaurs aren't the only danger Derek Steel faces when he travels to 100 million BC. Saboteurs try to prevent the terra-forming of Mars. They don't realize the consequences it will have if they are successful. Will Derek find his lover again or will they both be lost on the Cliffs of Time?

Orion – The Hunt

Hektor Orion joins the Hunt on Izzard-Junction to find his kidnapped mind-sister Delina. Stranded in the deep jungle of a hostile planet, the motley members of the hunting party must find their way back to civilization, but freedom may not be at the end of their journey.

http://www.hegro.blogspot.com/

Herbert Grosshans is the Author of 'The Xandra' trilogy and the 'Seeds of Chaos' series. He has also published a number of short stories which appeared in various digests from Midnight Showcase Fiction. His first story 'The Anniversary Gift' was part of the 'Sweet Revenge' digest. Then came 'Remember Me Next Christmas' in Holiday Voices, 'Gin and Tonic' in Summer Heat 3, 'Orola, the Kiir' in Midnight Raunch, and 'For Love of Arilee' in Sweet Challenge. Book One of 'Stardogs, Return to Redsky' is now available, followed by Book Two, 'Redemption', releasing in Spring 2008.

Herb's books can now be found at www.melange-books.com. Or see a list on his site.

The Cliffs of Time
by Herbert Grosshans

Chapter One

"After this morning's incident, nobody leaves the compound without at least one armed guard." André Pireux glared at the handful of supervisors sitting at the table in his boardroom. "As director of this facility, I'm responsible for every person and every piece of equipment."

He locked eyes with the small dark-skinned man standing at the end of the long table. "Dr. Bashir, you've been here longer than any of us. I expected you to be more aware of the dangers we face out there."

The little man pulled on his goatee. "You are absolutely correct, Director. I should have been more careful." He smiled. "As you pointed out, I've been here a long time. Ten years, to be precise. Two years without being up-line. I needed to get away from this place for a while, breathe natural air, smell the flowers and the soil, swim in a real pond and see animals in their natural environment."

"And provide a snack for the beasts that live in that natural environment," Pireux sneered. "If I hadn't immediately sent out a team to rescue you from the jaws of that Tyrannosaurus, you wouldn't stand here now."

"Carcharodontosaurus," Dr. Bashir said softly.

"What?"

"It was a Carcharodontosaurus. Tyrannosaurus rex won't appear for another thirty million years, or so."

Pireux made an impatient gesture. "Whatever that huge lizard is called." He sighed. "You're lucky I consider you such a valuable member of the research team, otherwise I might just have left you out there."

Dr. Bashir made a small bow. "I thank you for that

compassion, Director Pireux. Maybe some day I can pay you back. Are we done here? I'm a busy man."

"We're done. Go and do whatever you do."

The small man turned to leave. Hesitating, he stopped. "Oh, before I go, I'd like to remind you that I represent the Wells Foundation. Let me also refresh your memory. The Wells Foundation spearheaded this project and is funding a large part of it."

Director Pireux heaved another loud sigh. "How can I ever forget, Dr. Bashir? You remind me twice a month, at the very least."

When the door closed behind the little man, Pireux threw up his hands. Looking at the big man who sat on his right, he said, "Sorry about this, Mr. Steel, but that man has been a thorn in my side ever since I assumed my position as director of this project."

The big man smiled thinly. In the past two week, he'd seen tempers fly more than once. Most of the researchers and technicians didn't last much longer than a year before this place got to them. It had taken him a few days to adjust his mental state to the fact that he had traveled one hundred million years into the past. If, for some reason, he died in this place, archeologists digging in the soil for a peek into the past of Earth wouldn't find a trace of his existence, not even his fancy golden watch.

He smiled and thought, You wouldn't be too happy, Grandfather, if your treasured watch ended up in a time before it was made, buried under tons of granite, instead of being handed down to my oldest son. If I ever have one.

"We've had some valuable research data destroyed by a virus that suddenly popped up in our computer."

Steel brought his attention back to the people seated at the table and let his eyes rest on the older man across from him. "I know a little bit about computers," he said. "How can a virus even get into yours? This facility is totally isolated and removed from anything even vaguely electronic." He smiled. "One hundred million years removed. I'm still trying to get used to it." He looked at the others. "As I understand, every piece of electronic equipment is built and checked by computers up-line. No human hand touches any of the components. Not even the programs."

The older man gave Steel an almost hostile look. "Well, either the equipment doesn't get checked out as thoroughly as you think, or somebody in this compound is fooling around with the computers." He looked around the table at the anxious faces of his colleagues. "We have a saboteur among us."

"A saboteur?" A young woman beside him laughed. "Now you're becoming just a little bit too paranoid, Dr. Olfson. Everyone here has been investigated from top to bottom. The government knows more about each one of us than we do ourselves." She shook her long blond hair. "No, Dr. Olfson, you're wrong. Not even a pregnant mouse gets into the base without being investigated first."

Some of the others laughed.

"The last thing we need here in the Mesozoic era is a pregnant mouse. No telling what her descendants would look like in the twenty-first century AD."

Steel studied the man who made that comment. He didn't look like a researcher. Tall and muscular, he could have been a model for a men's clothing catalogue. *There is something arrogant about this man, I'm not sure if I like him.* When he looked up, he noticed the young blond woman's stare. She seemed to study him intensely.

"I haven't seen you before, Mr. Steel. What exactly is your job here?" It sounded like an innocent question, but Steel had the impression it was more than just rhetorical.

"I'm here to check out your computers." Steel gave her a smile. "I didn't get your name and your position."

"I'm Captain Gifford, and I'm the head of the local constabulary." She smiled back at him, but her blue eyes stayed cool. Then she looked at Director Pireux. "Why wasn't I made aware of Mr. Steel's arrival? Security in this place is not taken seriously. I'm almost inclined to assume Dr. Olfson's attitude."

"I saw no reason to notify you of Mr. Steel's arrival. He is no security threat." Director Pireux made an impatient gesture of dismissal. "This meeting is over."

When Steel rose from his seat, Pireux said, "I'd like to have a word with you, Mr. Steel." He turned to the blond woman. "You, too, Captain Gifford."

When everyone left, the Director leaned back in his chair, looked first at Steel and then at the woman. "I apologize if I waited for you to meet, but even you, Captain Gifford, are not above suspicion."

Gifford lifted an eyebrow. "Meaning what, Director?"

"Meaning I take no chances with anyone, unless I know them personally." He paused. "Captain Gifford, let me introduce you to Lt. Derek Steel, Special Investigator with Army Intelligence."

"I thought you were a computer expert."

Steel smiled. "I am."

"I see." Her eyes flashed back to Pireux. "I didn't like that remark about me not being above suspicion, Director Pireux. I'm the head of security, for heaven's sake. If you can't trust me…?

Pireux cut her off. "I take it back." He smiled at Steel. "She's quite competent, Lieutenant, but has a bit of a temper. Watch her."

Gifford shook her head and rolled her eyes. "If I didn't know any better, I'd say you hate me, Director."

Pireux chuckled. "How can anyone hate a beautiful woman like you, Gifford?"

The woman's blue eyes clouded over. "I know I shouldn't get angry over that remark, because you mean it as a compliment, but I wish you would see me as a professional first and a woman second." She glanced at Steel. "Is the lieutenant reporting to me, or is he an independent?"

"He reports to me, Captain. Lt. Steel's identity will not be revealed to anyone. As far as everyone else is concerned, he is a computer expert, here to check out the computers."

"So why reveal his identity to me?"

The Director smiled. "Because I trust you, Captain Gifford."

Chapter Two

The huge rock formation jutting into the mouth of the river took the brunt of the choppy water rushing into the ocean and created a relatively quiet bay behind its jagged and steep cliffs.

Steel watched in silence as the few passengers boarded the boat, taking them upriver to Station Zeta, which housed the laboratories and the launch pads for the rockets.

Two guards stood by the shore, watching the sky and the water, their weapons ready. A flock of what looked like giant birds circled above the cliffs.

Steel inhaled deeply, finding it difficult to breathe in the hot humid air. It was laden with sulfur and the pungent odor of dung. Dinosaur dung.

"Are you waiting to be carried away by one of those Pterodactyls?"

He turned to look at the blond woman stepping out of the armored vehicle and smiled. "Morning, Captain Gifford. I'm just enjoying the view," he said. "I've never seen anything like it, since I spent most of my life in the ghettos of New York and in army barracks."

"The view might be spectacular, but so are the predators." She grabbed his arm. "Come, let's get into the safety of the boat. You never know when those flying reptiles decide to have lunch."

"They don't look that big."

She laughed. "You better hope you never get a front row seat to see how big they really are. Some of them have a wingspan of over twenty five feet, and their teeth are sharp."

The wide plank connecting the boat to shore swayed slightly when Steel stepped onto it, and he grabbed the railing for support. The boat didn't have an open deck. A transparent dome covered it from bow to stern.

"Are you sure we're safe in this thing?" Steel asked.

"Quite sure," Gifford said. "The canopy is built from plasteel, and the hull is covered with two inches of titanium alloy. Any beastie trying to gobble us up will literally break its teeth. On top

8

of that, we are armed with missile-throwers. They'll knock down anything we've encountered so far."

They took their seats in the back on the top deck. Only four other passengers sat in the front, the others climbed down the steep stairs to the deck below.

"This is quite a large boat," Steel commented.

"It has the capacity to carry forty passengers, plus a crew of six. Then there is, of course, the storage area for luggage and supplies."

"How far is Station Zeta?"

"Almost twenty miles on the river." She made herself comfortable in her seat. "Here we go. We're moving. Might as well relax."

Steel felt the gentle swaying of the boat and the muffled sounds of the engine. He watched the rocky cliffs go by on his right. When the boat passed the tongue of land and the high waves smashed into it, it began rocking violently, but only for a moment, until they faced into the strong current.

"Is the river always this wild?"

"Most of the time. This is a violent era in the history of our planet."

Inhaling the cool and fresh air blowing at him from one of the air vents, he felt grateful for the air conditioning. His damp clothes clung to his body from the humid outside air. "Dr. Bashir babbled something about smelling the natural air outside," he said, chuckling. "I never did find the smell of sulfur pleasant."

"It's the volcanoes. They're constantly erupting, spewing all that pleasant aroma into the air." Gifford laughed, wrinkling her nose. "I'm not that fond of the smell from the tons and tons of droppings the dinosaurs leave behind."

Steel turned his head to look at her. "I like the way you laugh," he said and smiled.

"You do?"

"Yes, I do. Actually, I find you quite attractive. Are you married?"

"I don't think that's any of your business, Derek…Mr. Steel." She sounded frosty and almost upset. And sad.

"Did I say something wrong?" he asked.

"You talk just like Director Pireux and most of the men I have to deal with. It would be nice to be treated as an equal. Is that all you see in me…a woman?"

Steel smiled. "How can I not see a woman? You are a woman…and a beautiful one on top of that. Let me ask you a question. What do you see when you look at me?"

She hesitated. "A man, I guess." She smiled suddenly and then laughed. "A handsome, good-looking man."

"Thank you. I have no problem with that. By the way, my first name is Derek."

"I know." Her face clouded over again, but then she smiled. "Maybe living here this long is beginning to affect me. Lately, everything irritates me. Call me Melanie."

"Hi, Melanie." He held out his hand. "I've been here only three weeks, and I feel lonely already. I could use a friend."

She looked at him with a strange expression on her beautiful face. "I know. It gets lonely here. I could be your…friend."

"How long have you been here?" he asked.

"Nearly two years. It seems like ten." She sighed. "My job as head of security is boring, to say the least. Not much exiting ever happens." She chuckled. "Occasionally a brawl breaks out in the lounge, usually among the technicians after they drank too much. I can't even get involved in them. My men take care of those things. Sometimes, I have the feeling they enjoy it. Can't say I blame them."

"If you need some action, maybe you and I can have a go at it in the gym. I'm a fair martial artist," he said, half jokingly.

"Kung Fu? Karate?" she asked.

"Wing Chun Kung Fu."

"You're on," she said, chuckling. "Don't be surprised if I beat the pants off you…Derek."

"I can hardly wait." He grinned.

"How are your computers behaving these days?" Melanie asked.

Steel shrugged. "Right now I'm in the process of comparing the list of people who are working here with the list of names of the people who stepped into the time-transporter between 2065 AD and 2085 AD. The ones who have returned home in those twenty years have already been investigated. I have discovered a few discrepancies, but I haven't drawn any conclusions, yet. I'm hoping it's just sloppy record keeping. What do you know about Akim Rocksal? I met him that morning in the boardroom."

Melanie chuckled. "Akim Rocksal, the Hunk. All the women worship him. He's the head of Evaluations. Why do you ask about him?"

"His name is not on my list."

"What does that mean?" She stared at him.

"According to my records, he didn't come here through the time-transporter. He doesn't exist."

"That's impossible. How did he get here?"

"Like I said, hopefully just some glitch in the records. There are two more people who apparently don't exist."

"Who?"

"One Terry Scott, a technician in Station Zeta. I'm planning to look him up when we get there."

"And the other one?"

Steel didn't look at her, but he could feel her eyes on him. "Someone in the Alpha Complex."

"Who?" she asked again.

"I don't know. Before I could get the information, some sophisticated spy program wiped the memory web on my c-chip. Whoever did this, knows more about computer programming than I do. And I'm considered an expert."

Melanie stayed silent. After a while, she said, "You were present when I laughed off Dr. Olfson's suggestion we might have a saboteur on the Station, but you know, he is right. We do have a saboteur amongst us. I just don't want to create a panic. We've had two mysterious explosions before this last one in Station Zeta, damaging a number of critical components beyond repair. Apparently, they set back the project for months."

"I have no reports on that."

"No, you don't. They were never filed."

"Why not?"

She chuckled. "It takes a lot of money to keep this place going. We don't want to scare off the investors."

Steel filed away this information. He already knew about the explosions. It was the last information the *Watchdog* sent upline. "You've had an accident recently. A man got killed," he said.

Melanie sighed. "Yes," she said. "One of the computer people by the name of Abram Stettman. He was crushed to death. A crate fell on him when he checked out a problem with the lifts in Station Zeta. I filed a detailed report."

"I know. I read it." Steel looked up into the sky and at the tops of the giant trees, wondering what kind of creatures lived in their thick branches, and below them. Mammals didn't exist in this epoch. They wouldn't appear for another few millions of years. Reptiles ruled the Mesozoic era. Humans tried to intrude into their kingdom, tried to play god. Who knew what the repercussions of this interference would be. "Maybe we're not supposed to be here," he said. "Sometimes, things should be left the way they are."

She looked at him strangely. "Perhaps," she murmured.

Chapter Three

Tall and skeletal, his face a pallid color, Professor Darking looked like a man death rejected, but he didn't act like someone back from the dead. His enthusiasm for the project showed clearly in his surprisingly strong voice.

"They tell me you're the genius behind Project Mars," Steel said to him.

The Professor laughed. "You're giving me too much credit, Mr. Steel. It's true, I came up with the idea, but there are many other smart people involved."

"What exactly are you hoping to achieve?"

"Create life on Mars. Surely you're familiar with the project."

"I am, but I'd like to hear it from you." Steel chuckled. "Like getting a valuable book signed by its author."

Darking smiled. "You want the long or the short version?"

"The short one will do. I probably wouldn't understand the long one."

"Well, as everyone knows, Mars is a dead planet in our present timeline. Nothing but sand and rocks. Earth is overpopulated. Too many people on our shrinking world. Even they Great War of Armageddon in 2012 didn't put a dent big enough into the number of people on our planet, even though we lost over a billion lives. Humans are breeding more vigorously than ever. Mars would be an ideal world to relieve the crowded conditions.

"It takes millions of years to terra-form a planet. Time we don't have. So when the researchers of the Wells Foundation discovered a way to travel back in time, I came up with the idea of starting the terra-forming process in the past." Professor Darking beamed happily. "Really just a logical solution."

"How can you accomplish that?"

"Our first step is to establish a research station on Mars. Actually, we do have six men and six women already living on Mars for the past three years. Mars is not a dead planet in one hundred million BC. We have air, breathable air."

"So why the need to terra-form Mars?"

"Because the planet is dead one hundred million years from now. We don't know exactly why. There are theories, of course, but that's all they are, theories. We need to know for certain what killed the red planet."

"How can you find out?"

"By going into the future. This future. We've almost finished building a time-transporter on Mars."

"I thought that traveling into the future is not possible, unless a terminal already exists."

Darking smiled congenially. "We will have one on Mars in the year 2086."

"I didn't know that," Steel said, making a mental note to talk to the people who sent him here.

"Have you found out what causes the problem with the computers?" the Professor asked.

"Not yet."

Darking looked at his watch. "If you'll excuse me, Mr. Steel, I have something urgent to check out."

He must be at least a hundred years old, Steel thought as he watched the old man shuffle away. *I guess his pet project keeps him alive.* He turned and headed for the elevator.

Time to talk to Terry Scott, the technician.

Before he reached the elevator, he changed his mind and walked over to one of the large windows. A huge expanse of nothing but savannah stretched toward the horizon, broken up by mountains of giant rocks. From his position on the fifth floor, the grass covering the land looked short, but he knew it grew ten feet tall and provided cover for all sizes of predators.

Everything in this epoch was huge. If primitive humans existed in this period, they didn't stand a chance against the forever hungry and ferocious beasts that ruled the land, the jungle and the oceans. And don't forget the sky, he thought as he watched a flock of giant winged reptiles soaring above the jungle to his left. He saw the river snaking its way toward the mountains in the west. The sun burned down from the hazy sky. A few dark clouds hovered over the mountains, promising rain. He shuddered. The Earth he knew didn't look like this in the year 2085 AD. The jungle he knew was paved with concrete, and the trees were giant skyscrapers reaching toward the heavens.

"Here you are! I've been looking for you."

He turned at the sound of Melanie's voice and watched her walking toward him. The tight fitting uniform she wore molded itself around her slim but muscular arms and legs. The wide gun-belt accentuated her narrow waist.

A sudden fluttering in his loins made him aware that he had been a long time without a woman.

If she noticed him studying her, she didn't remark on it. He smiled. Maybe she was beginning to tolerate him.

"How did your talk with Professor Darking go?" she asked.

"As well as expected." He shrugged. "Except for a couple of things, he didn't really tell me anything I didn't know already."

"Why did you bother talking to him?"

"Courtesy, I guess. After all, he is the head of Station Zeta." He looked at her, bewitched by her beautiful smile.

Damn! he thought. I can't let her beauty cloud my thinking and impartiality. Why couldn't she have been a man? Or ugly?

"Something wrong?" she asked.

Shaking his head, he said, "No. I was just thinking. Nothing important. What about your investigation into the explosion?"

"One of the biologists got injured when the section of the lab that housed his cultures blew up. Nothing serious, but his research has gone up in smoke, literally." She looked out of the window and at the moving dark clouds. "Looks like a storm is coming. They can be spectacular…and scary."

"I was just about to go talk to Terry Scott. Want to come?" Steel gave her an inquiring look.

"Okay," she said. "Got nothing else planned."

Scott turned out to be in his thirties. He could have been handsome, had it not been for his height. Five foot, one inch. Steel had read it in his file.

"Hi, Terry," Steel addressed him, smiling. "I'm Derek Steel. I just got here from upline. I'm checking out the problem with the computers."

"So?" The man looked suddenly wary.

"I'd like to ask you a few questions."

"Like what?"

"Well, like, how long have you been here?"

"A few months."

"Ninety six days, actually," Steel said.

Scott gave him a defiant look. "If you knew that, why did you ask me?"

Steel smiled. "I wanted *you* to tell me. Funny thing, I can't find your name in the records upline."

"Then how do you know about me?" Scott stared up at Steel and then at Melanie. "Are you going to arrest me because of some computer glitch?"

"Nobody is arresting you, Mr. Scott," Melanie said. "We're just here to ask you some questions."

"You did, and I answered them. Are we finished?"

"Not quite. Do you know anything about computers, Terry?" Steel asked.

"As much as anyone else. Why?"

"Just wondering. How about building a bomb? You know how?"

"What?" Scott shook his head. "What kind of a stupid question is that?"

"Are you familiar with the components of a temporal device?" Melanie asked.

Scott threw her a startled look, his eyes narrowed. "I have no idea what you're talking about. I'm just a technician, not a scientist," he said and threw up both hands. "I'm finished with you."

"We'll be in touch, Mr. Scott," Melanie called after him.

"What was that about a temporal device?" Steel asked her.

She shrugged and smiled. "Nothing really. I thought it might throw him off guard." She grabbed Steel's arm. "Come on, let's get something to eat. I hear their chef makes a good dinosaur steak."

Chapter Four

"I think I drank a little too much." Melanie giggled and hung onto Steel's arm.

"A little?" Steel chuckled. "I believe you're drunk, Miss Gifford."

"Maybe. But just a teeny weenie bit." She giggled again. "And don't call me Miss Gifford. My friends call me Melanie." She hiccupped. "You know, it's been a long time since I went on a date with a man. Much too long."

Steel laughed. "I didn't know we were on a date. I should have dressed for the occasion."

"We weren't?" She stopped and moved in front of him. "If you would ask me if you could kiss me, I would let you." She put a finger against his lips. "Maybe I'll kiss you instead."

Before she could say more, Steel took her face between his hands and looked into her blue eyes. They didn't seem cold at all. Her teeth shone white in her half-open mouth. He could smell the liqueur on her warm breath. Bending down, he pressed his lips against hers. She responded by opening her mouth and pushing her tongue between his teeth.

Laughing into his mouth, she molded her body into his. Then she broke the kiss and grabbed his hand. "Come," she said huskily, her breath coming fast, "before I change my mind."

There was nobody in the elevator, and she flung herself into his arms the moment the doors closed. They kissed until the elevator stopped.

"I prefer my room," she said and pulled him with her. Once inside the room, she unbuckled her gun belt and let it fall to the floor. Then she unzipped her uniform jacket.

Steel stood in silence as she removed her bra and watched her breasts tumble out. Proud and solid, as he expected. "You're a beautiful and seductive woman," he said, his breath catching in his throat.

"Now you." She looked at him from lowered lashes. Her hand went behind her head and undid the clasp that held back her long blond hair and let it tumble around her face.

He took off his jacket and slipped out of his shirt.

"Nice body," she murmured and came up to him. Her hands stroked his chest and his wide shoulders. She hooked one finger into his belt. "Are you built like this down there, too?"

He grinned. "Why not find out?"

With deft fingers, she undid his buckle, and then she slowly pulled down his zipper. Her hand found him before she even pushed down his pants. "Hard and thick," she mumbled, sinking to her knees. Her lips touched the swollen head of his penis, and her tongue swirled around the tip.

He groaned and grabbed a handful of her hair, letting her suck him deep into her warm mouth. He closed his eyes, enjoying the tantalizing pleasure as she teased the underside of his organ with her velvety tongue. Before he could come inside her mouth, she freed him and rose up in front of him, her breasts grazing his belly and then his chest. Becoming aware of his pants pooling around his ankles and his boots, he said hoarsely, "Let's get undressed."

She stepped back. With tormenting slowness, she hooked her fingers into her tight slacks and pushed them past her hips, exposing her flat belly and the blond fluffy triangle of her pussy. He could see the pink slit between her thick lips.

Pulling her slim legs out of her leggings, she stood in front of him, a wicked smile on her face. Then she turned and walked toward the bed. He watched the play of her round buttocks, admiring their perfect shape.

She lay down on the edge of the bed and opened her legs wide, giving him a good look at her pussy. "It won't bite you," she said and smiled, beckoning with a crooked finger.

He knelt between her spread thighs, and, with his finger, he opened the folds of her vagina. Gluing his mouth over her pussy, he began licking her tiny rigid member. She squealed with delight and closed her thighs against his head. "Oh, yes," she moaned. "You know exactly what I need. You always did." She came with a sharp cry, and he lapped up her warm juice.

Rising to his feet, he put his hard mast between her swollen labia, and pushing forward, he slid into her with ease. She cried out and began to buck violently. Putting his hands around her hips, he pulled her to him with every thrust.

She threw her head from side to side, a painful expression on her face. Dousing him several times with her warm discharge, she reached toward him with outstretched arms. "Welcome home," she whispered. "Come, let me cradle you between my thighs and feel your hard chest against my breasts."

He pulled out and waited until she moved up on the bed. Then he lay between her open thighs. She took him back into her and wrapped her long legs around his torso, resting her heels on his clenching buttocks.

"You feel so wonderful inside me," she whispered, slamming her hips up against his. "It's been so long."

He didn't answer, just concentrated on her softly rippling inner muscles and the pleasure he experienced holding her solid, but warm and yielding, body. When he knew he couldn't hold back any longer, he dug his fingers into her soft buttocks and held her tight while he erupted inside her with the force of an exploding volcano.

She raked his back with her long fingers and let out a series of suppressed cries, milking him violently. "Oh, my sweet darling," she sobbed, "I've waited so long for you. I've missed this so much."

After it was over, he relaxed into her embrace, trying to catch his breath.

"I thought you were trying to kill me with that weapon of yours," she said, still gasping for air.

"Did I hurt you?" he asked, concerned.

She laughed. "If pleasure is pain, then, yes, you hurt me terribly."

He kissed her gently. "I can't remember when someone made me feel this good," he said.

She stroked his cheek with gentle fingers. "You've made me very happy, too." Then she pushed against his chest. "You're getting heavy."

He rolled to her side and lay there, studying her face. "You are so beautiful," he said. His hand cupped her breast. "And your body is perfectly formed."

"I work out." She chuckled. "To have a fit and healthy body is a great asset in my job."

"Speaking of assets," he said and laughed. "You have a beautiful ass, too."

"Oh, you," she chided and slapped him playfully. Running a finger down the crease between her breasts, she said, "I'm slick with sweat. And so are you."

"I guess we should take a shower. Maybe it'll sober up both of us."

"I'm not drunk," she said and hiccupped. She giggled. "Not much, anyway."

He slipped off the bed and padded toward the shower cubicle.

"Your ass isn't so bad either," she called after him and laughed.

When he came out of the shower, she was asleep. He covered her up with the thin blanket and kissed her on the cheek. Then he dressed and went to his own room just down the hall.

I hope neither one of us feels awkward in the morning, he thought as he crawled into his bed.

Chapter Five

Melanie seemed cheerful and chipper at breakfast. "Slept well?" she asked him, a twinkle in her blue eyes.

Steel smiled. "I had a wonderful dream," he said.

"So did I. I hope I'll have one like that again, soon." She reached across the table and touched his hand. "I know this is crazy, and it's happening a little too fast, but I'm in love with you, Derek." She gave him a shy smile. When Steel stayed silent, she took her hand away and sighed. "You don't have to say anything. I'm sorry if I blab like a lovesick teenager, and I apologize if I make you feel uncomfortable." She smiled lopsidedly. "Maybe it's the air. Or maybe I just needed a good fuck."

He looked at her and reached out to touch her cheek. "I have feelings for you, too, Melanie. Maybe last night happened a little sooner than it should have, maybe I took advantage of your intoxicated state, but I'm not sorry it happened. We're both adults. I'm a little surprised you feel the way you do. Somehow, I had the impression you didn't like me."

"I liked you the first time I saw you." She smiled happily. "Sometimes, I have a hard time letting others see my true feelings. Even now I'm still a little scared."

"Somebody hurt you?"

She nodded. "Not intentionally. He…left me, but not out of choice. Circumstances beyond our control ripped us apart. I've been lonely since. I loved him very much."

"You still love him?"

Her eyes were large and moist when she looked at him. "I love *you*, Derek," she said softly, touching his hand again. "How about you? Anyone special in you life?"

"Me?" He shrugged. "I was married once. It didn't work out. I got over it."

Liar, he thought. *You never get over it when you love a woman so much it hurts, and then you find her screwing your best friend. Never!*

"The boat won't leave until tomorrow." Melanie seemed all

bubbly. "I'd like to take you on a tour. There is something I want you to see."

After breakfast, they went down to Operations and requested a rover, one of those small armored two-seaters. Shaped like a teardrop, it floated on a cushion of air and could reach speeds of over one hundred miles an hour.

"If we can't outrun them, we'll blow 'em up," Melanie joked, when Steel commented on the small rocket launcher on top of the roof.

"What kind of predators are you expecting?" he asked.

"None, I hope."

The bad storm Melanie seemed worried about never materialized. A strong wind from the east blew the dark clouds back into the mountains. Melanie kept the rover skimming the tall grass.

"This is about as high as I can safely take it," she explained. "Higher than this and this thing will begin to wobble all over the place."

When Steel glanced at the speedometer, he noticed their speed. Melanie saw him looking.

"We could go much faster, but I consider anything above fifty miles unsafe," she said and smiled. "I know, the rolling surface of this ocean of grass just invites you to race across it, but it's too dangerous. One of the boys from the geology department almost killed himself when he collided with an Acanthopholis. At one hundred and twenty miles an hour, objects come up pretty fast. Speed can be deadly, even here in the Cretaceous period."

"Did he survive?"

"He did. He's fine, except for a sprained neck and some broken ribs where the seatbelt cut into his chest. These rovers can stand a lot of abuse, humans can't."

"I'm talking about the Acanthopholis," Steel said and grinned.

"Oh." She laughed. "He survived. Those Ankylosaurs are heavily armored and weigh up to four hundred kilograms. I'm sure he's got quite a headache, though."

"It looks so peaceful," Steel commented, looking out of the

rover's tinted window. "I find it strange not to see the sky swarming with air-cars and planes. And this vast area covered with just grass. It's overwhelming. The only empty lands I've seen were the deserts of Africa, the desolate blackened earth and the scorched craters of West Asia and Southern Europe, still uninhabitable since the Great War of Armageddon."

"I've never seen it," Melanie said. "It must have been terrible, that war. To think people murdered their fellow human beings just because they had a different faith. I can't even imagine such lunacy."

"Neither can I." He smiled sadly. "But we still kill each other, only for different reasons. I don't think that will ever change. Humans are predatory, as predatory and ferocious as those dinosaurs out there."

The topography changed gradually. They flew over a large body of water. Tall reed-like grasses covered great sections of swamp, and Steel saw a number of large scaly backs protruding from the water.

"Those are Theropods," Melanie said. "Probably trying to catch some fish. But fish isn't their only diet. They are fast and agile bipedal carnivores and smart."

"I'm glad I'm protected inside this vehicle," Steel said, laughing, "Wouldn't want to face those oversized lizards unarmed."

"You don't want to face any of these scaly beasts…armed or unarmed. Even the small ones are ferocious and can inflict terrible wounds, probably kill you."

"How safe is this rover?" Steel asked.

"Safe. Don't worry. They're practically indestructible."

In the hazy distance, Steel could see high mountains, their peaks lost in the clouds.

After skimming over the flat surface for two hours, they left the swamp behind and flew alongside a forest of tall and massive trees, most of them conifers of some kind. Melanie brought the rover down beside a rushing river which originated somewhere in the mountains and continued on its way into forest.

"Take one of these," she told Steel and reached behind their seats to pull out a heavy-looking short-barreled rifle.

"Are we expecting trouble?" he asked.

"Out there? Always be on guard," she warned him.

The hot, humid air took Steel's breath away for a moment, and the overpowering stench assaulted his nostrils. Then he became aware of the noisy environment. Roaring, hissing, the shrill cry of the smaller reptilian creatures and the buzzing of swarms of insects left his ears ringing.

"I think I prefer the noise of a city to this," he called to Melanie. "And the smell, too." Slapping at the insects that began settling on his exposed face and neck, he cursed when one of them stung him.

Melanie reached into her shoulder bag and handed him a small tube. "Rub this over your skin." She took out another tube and applied its contents to her face and hands. Then she laughed and spread her arms. "I love the freedom and the wide open spaces. I get claustrophobic in the concrete jungles of my time." She became serious. "Watch the sky, the tree tops and the high grass. And the river. Some nasty critters lurk in its murky depth."

They walked toward the river, wary and watchful. A loud roar from the forest made Steel jerk around and lift his rifle.

"Sounds like a Giganotosaurus is in the vicinity."

"Giganotosaurus?"

"The forerunner of the Tyrannosaurus rex. Larger, but lighter in built, and not quite as smart, but just as deadly and dangerous."

"Sounds like a fun fellow to run into," Steel joked.

"I hope not."

Carefully stepping around a large boulder, Melanie stopped and waited for Steel to join her. What he saw made him let out a sharp whistle. "These shouldn't be here," was all he could say.

Melanie smiled grimly. "No, they shouldn't be, but here they are."

Steel stared at the six oblong rocks sticking out of the ground in one straight row. They were overgrown with slimy lichens, except for a couple of spots, where someone had wiped off some of the green slime to expose rough letters chiseled into the rock's surface.

"Remos Flandry," he read and looked at Melanie. "They look weathered. I'm guessing forty, maybe fifty years old. I don't understand."

"I figure they've been here for at least seventy years," Melanie said.

"But no humans lived in this age, not in one hundred million BC."

"As far as we know. But this tells us different."

"Primitive humanoids could never survive in this environment, not with all these huge meat eaters everywhere." Steel shook his head.

"They weren't primitives, Derek. These people possessed tools."

"Looks that way, and tools mean weapons, but to reach this stage takes possibly thousands of years. They could never have survived that long. There must be another explanation." He smiled. "Besides, what primitive humanoid would be called Remos Flandry?"

"You're right." Melanie returned his smile. "I never suggested that we're dealing with primitive people." She stared at him. "There is another explanation. Others have been here before us. Others who traveled back in time."

"Wonder what happened. Maybe they became stranded and perished here."

"You might be right," Melanie agreed.

"How did you discover these graves?"

"Purely by chance. I accompanied one of the geologists on a research mission, and we sort of stumbled across them. At first, we thought they were just an interesting rock formation, until we wiped off the lichens."

"Where, or more precisely when, would these time travelers come from?" Steel asked.

Melanie shrugged. "Most likely from a time in our future."

"You'd think by then traveling trough time would be perfected," Steel mused.

"I'm only assuming," Melanie said. "Maybe they came from another timeline."

"Timeline?"

"Yes." She gave him a long look. "What do you think happens if this Mars-project succeeds?"

Steel lifted his shoulders. "Humans will have another planet to populate?"

"Possibly. It also means that this timeline we're in will become unstable, and reality will shift into another shadow-line. Anything done in the past will have repercussions in the future. We will change the future."

Steel looked at her in surprise. "Shadow-lines? I've never heard that term before. Have you suddenly become an expert in time-travel?"

"I've studied Professor Darking's theories. I told you, life down here can be boring."

Steel scrutinized the gravestones again. "Somebody buried these people. Where are the survivors?"

"Dead by now," Melanie said. "If the dinosaurs didn't eat them, and if they somehow managed to survive and die of natural causes, the scavengers left no traces of their passing."

A loud splash from the direction of the river made them both turn. A huge crocodile-like amphibian started climbing on land, surveying its surroundings with glittering eyes and open jaws.

"Someone is looking for a meal," Steel said. "I'd say we make a hasty retreat."

"I agree." Melanie held her rifle ready and took a few steps backwards into the protection of the large boulder. Steel followed her example. Once past the boulder and out of the creature's sight, they turned and began jogging back to their vehicle.

"Keep your eyes open," Melanie warned.

Steel breathed a sigh of relief when they stood beside the rover.

"Get in!" Melanie said. "I think our new friend is following us."

When Steel looked back the way they had come, he saw the huge bulk of the giant amphibian heading toward them with alarming speed.

Once inside the rover, Melanie made sure the doors were

secured, and then she strapped herself into her seatbelts, urging Steel to hurry up. He finished with his, leaned back in his seat and said, "Let's get out of here!"

When Melanie engaged the power leaver, nothing happened. She cursed and looked at Steel. "We have a problem."

"What?" He stared past her at the beast approaching them. It looked even larger that close. The teeth in its open jaws seemed capable of piercing the hull of their vehicle.

"Damn thing won't start!" Melanie cursed.

"Can you fix it?"

She shrugged inside her web of belts. "Don't know."

The rover shook and lurched sideways as the reptilian creature rammed it with great force. Steel stared into the huge maw when the creature attempted to sink its teeth into the hard shell of the vehicle. Melanie tried again to start the motor but failed.

"Can't you blast this thing with our rocket launcher?" Steel yelled.

"Not without power."

"I thought this rover was indestructible?"

"The outer shell is," Melanie yelled back and banged her fist into the dashboard. "This is not happening!"

The rover lurched again as their attacker rammed it with its bony head. When Melanie pulled the power leaver for a third time, a few lights began to glow on the control board and the motor sprang to life, but when she tried to move the rocket launcher into position, it wouldn't respond.

"Damn animal must have bent our canon," she cursed loudly. "Maybe we can escape."

The amphibian pulled back for another assault. Melanie used the opportunity to turn the rover. It responded sluggishly and barely moved when she pushed the accelerator. Their giant opponent clamped its massive jaws around their vehicle again.

"I'll have to try something else." She pushed a couple of buttons, and suddenly the outside of the rover lit up like a Christmas tree. "Maybe this will get your attention!" Melanie shouted.

A shudder went through the rover. Melanie worked the controls and managed to free it from the creature's jaws. When Steel looked, he saw the giant reptile convulsing on the ground.

"Ten thousand volts will do that," Melanie said triumphantly and grinned at Steel, but then she cursed again. "I think we are dead in the water," she said.

"Meaning?" Steel asked.

"That last desperate try to get us free killed the power supply. That should not have happened. I'm beginning to suspect we've been sabotaged." She peered at the unmoving behemoth outside. Then she carefully unlocked the door and opened it. Unstrapping herself, she eased out of the door. "I think it's safe," she said to Steel, reached into the vehicle and pressed a couple of buttons on the dashboard. A panel in the front of the rover snapped open.

Steel joined her outside, and they both stared at the exposed components and mass of wires.

"There," Steel said and pointed at a fused bundle of black wires and the charred remains of a rectangular plastic box. He scraped the box with a finger and smelled the powdered scrapings. "A timed explosive device," he commented and looked at Melanie. "You're right, somebody tampered with this vehicle."

Melanie climbed back into the rover. She came out a few moments later. "The comm is dead. We're on our own."

"How far back to the base?" Steel asked.

"About one hundred and thirty miles, give or take a few miles. Too far to walk. We'll never make it." She looked up into the sky and then back into the nearby jungle.

Steel was suddenly aware of the roaring and hissing all around them. A flock of flying reptiles circled in the air currents above them. He could almost hear the beating of the giant leathery wings. He looked at the unmoving huge amphibian beside their vehicle.

Melanie saw him look. "If you think this is bad, wait until night. That's when the big ones come out."

"So what do we do?"

"We seek shelter elsewhere." She went back to the rover and pulled out her backpack, shouldered it and grabbed the big rifle.

Then she looked at the mountain ridge in the east. "It's only about ten miles to the foot of the mountains. We have a good chance to make it there."

"And then what?"

She smiled. "We'll find shelter there. Come." She started to walk away.

Steel followed her, his rifle in both hands, ready to be used.

Chapter Six

Traveling through the tall grass proved to be rough. They walked without talking, trying to be as silent as possible. Melanie followed a compass, which she had dug out of her backpack. Without it they surely would have walked in circles because at times the grass grew so tall, it made navigating extremely difficult.

After about thirty minutes of walking, Melanie stopped and studied a small device she held in her hand. "I think we've picked up company," she said with a low voice.

Steel looked at the small screen and saw a number of moving dots.

"What do these dots mean?" he asked.

Melanie pointed at two stationary dots. "You and me," she whispered. "Those others? Hunters."

"Who are they hunting?"

"Us."

"What are they?"

She shrugged. "I can't tell, but from my readings I assume they're Deinonychus. That means we're in trouble. They're smart and deadly predators, and they hunt in packs. They'll attack even large dinosaur. We have only one chance. We know where they are, and we wait for them to attack us. Get ready."

After trampling down the grass in a circle around them to give them a larger area to control, they stood back to back, waiting.

"One is heading straight for us from your direction," Melanie said calmly.

Steel heard the rustling of the grass, and then he faced the first of their hunters. He reacted without conscious thought. Bringing the rifle to his cheek, he aimed for the open jaws and pulled the trigger. The head of the saurian creature exploded, spraying Steel with blood and body matter. He didn't have much time for triumph. Behind the first one another one appeared, sharp, serrated teeth gleaming in its powerful jaws. Steel just kept on firing into the snapping maw.

Behind him, he heard Melanie's rifle firing and felt her back slam into his from the recoil of her rifle.

"Two o'clock!" she screamed.

Steel swung his rifle to his right, fired into the broad chest of the predator. It kept on advancing, tearing up the air in front of it with its clawed three-fingered hands. He put an exploding bullet into the gaping maw. The creature dropped to the ground, clawed feet scrabbling for support.

Melanie fired again. "There is one more," she said, "from your direction."

He heard it before it came out of the tall grass. When he saw its shadowy form through the thick stems, he began firing. It dropped, still a few yards away from their position.

"I think that was the last one," Melanie said and relaxed behind him. "Come, let's move on quickly. The dead bodies will attract the scavengers. They're just as deadly."

Steel gave the bloody corpses a closer look. Two of the Deinonychus were at least ten feet long and stood about five feet high at the shoulders. They had curved, flexible necks and long, rigid tails. He noticed the five-inch long claw on the second toe and shuddered, thinking of the injuries they could have inflicted.

With one last look, he followed Melanie.

"If we're lucky," she said, "we may be safe for a while. The scavengers will be busy. Of course, we might always stumble across others."

"You're so cheerful," Steel said. "By the way, you seem to be quite knowledgeable when it comes to dinosaurs."

"I've spent a lot of time outside the compounds, accompanying some of the scientists. If you want to survive, you familiarize yourself with the dangers you may be facing. Most of the stuff I learned from Professor Reinstein." She laughed. "He must have lived in the time of the dinosaurs. He's a walking library, and he loves to lecture. All you have to do is listen, and you learn a lot."

"Perhaps he can give me some lessons," Steel said, chuckling.

"Didn't they brief you at all before they sent you down?"

Melanie asked.

"Actually, no." Steel shrugged. "They warned me against leaving the compound."

Melanie shook her head. "Unbelievable. At least I did get a crash course."

They walked on in silence. Steel noticed his feet beginning to drag and his clothing soaking with perspiration from the hot humid air. "How far still?" he asked Melanie.

"Maybe another half hour," she responded.

"Where are we actually going?"

"Let's not talk," she answered. "Save your strength."

"I could use some water."

"All right." She stopped and took off her backpack. "Here," she said, handing him a plastic bottle.

He took it gratefully and drank a little of the precious liquid. "A little warm," he said, smiling, "but tastes like the finest wine."

The grass became spare, and suddenly they left the savannah behind them.

"Over there." Melanie pointed to a steep cliff. "We may have to move fast," she said, looking into the sky.

Steel followed her gaze and saw the flock of dark shapes circling the cliffs.

Ahead of them lay a flat terrain, dotted with large boulders, sparse vegetation and a few clumps of tall trees.

"We could try to hide under those trees. Their branches are quite wide-spreading and should provide cover against predators from the sky," Steel suggested.

"They might also harbor predators of the tree-climbing variety," Melanie said with a wry smile.

"I guess we'll have to chance that."

Picking a lonely tree close by, they sprinted for it. Steel saw movement in the upper branches, but the small scaly creatures inhabiting the tree took flight before Steel and Melanie reached it.

"At least we know there aren't any larger beasts around," Steel panted as they squatted beside the thick trunk.

"There is something I need to tell you," Melanie said suddenly.

"That you're not human but a dinosaur in disguise?" Steel grinned.

Melanie smiled. "I'm glad you haven't lost your sense of humor."

"It's all I have to get me through this." He became serious. "Actually, I also need to tell you something."

"Maybe you should go first then."

"Remember when I told you about the names that didn't match up?"

"Yes."

"There was one more name I didn't mention. One other person who was not on my list." He looked at her gravely.

"I know. I wondered when you would tell me." Melanie's blue eyes searched his face. "That is the reason I need to talk to you now, before we get to that cliff."

"Who are you, Melanie?" he asked.

"Who I am is not important, but what I have to do here is vital."

"And what is that?"

"Let me explain something else first. The sudden malfunction of our rover. That was not an accident. Someone is trying to kill us." She laughed when he raised an eyebrow. "I don't need to tell you that, you probably guessed it already. Do you know why, though?"

"Because I'm investigating the malfunctioning computers?" Steel suggested. "Seems a little harsh, doesn't it?"

"It is, but you weren't really the target. I was."

"You? Why?"

"You know what Project Mars is all about. To create life on Mars. There are some people who don't want that to happen. They will do anything to prevent it from happening, including murder. I'm here to stop them."

Steel looked at her. "You're not just a security guard, I assume."

"No, I'm not. I'm a Time-agent from the year 2145 AD."

"Did you say 2145 AD?" Steel asked, doubt showing in his face. "Are you telling me you're from sixty years in my future?"

Melanie smiled. "In a way, but not exactly. I'm from a different timeline, a shadow-line, if the saboteurs are successful."

"I have a problem understanding that. I'm afraid I'm not an expert in time-travel."

"Neither am I. We've learned much since time-travel was discovered, and as well as traveling across the timelines."

"Now you're losing me. Traveling across timelines?"

"That's how we found out that humans will destroy Earth in the year 2140 AD if the Mars-project fails."

"And if it is successful?"

"Reality will shift into my timeline, making it stable. Humanity will still populate planet Earth in the year 2145 AD, and there will be peace between Mars and Earth."

Steel put his hand against his forehead. "This is a little too much information right now for me to digest. Peace between Earth and Mars? Was there a war?"

"In my timeline, Mars invaded Earth in the year 1950 AD. One third of Earth's population was exterminated and the survivors enslaved for one hundred and seventy years, until the year 2120, when Earth revolted against its masters. The revolution lasted ten years, with fighting going on at different parts of the globe. The cost in human life was high, an estimated seven hundred and fifty million humans died during that time. How many Martians died, is not known. Earth finally won the war. Now we exist in peace with our neighboring planet, a peace that will last for a long time."

Steel sat silent, his face in his hands, his eyes closed. When he opened them, he stared at Melanie, who had been watching him. "1950," he said slowly. "In my timeline…there was the Korean War, the war in Vietnam, the Gulf Wars in the Nineties and then finally the Great War of Armageddon in 2012…"

Melanie interrupted him. "None of them happened in my timeline."

"But you say Earth people were slaves for one hundred and seventy years, not to mention the cost in lives. Which is the better choice?"

"The choice is clear. In your timeline, Earth was destroyed."

"Who are these people who are trying to sabotage the Mars-project?"

"People from my own timeline, from the year 2070. They want to stop the terra-forming of Mars when it began, one hundred million BC."

"Why?"

"To prevent the Mars invasion from happening."

"A good reason."

"It is, except they don't know that they also doom planet Earth."

"Why don't they know?"

"Because they can't travel into the future."

"And you can?"

Melanie shook her head. "No, but I am from the future, their future. In my time, we know what happened, or, more precisely, what is possible."

Steel rose to his feet and stared into the cloudy sky. "This is hard for me to swallow. How can I believe you? Maybe your actions will bring even greater disasters."

Melanie stood beside him and touched his arm. "I'm not asking you to believe me. You will discover all this yourself. I'm just asking you to keep an open mind and remember everything I'm telling you. Promise me." She stepped in front of him and looked into his eyes. "And remember, I love you." Lifting up, she kissed him on the lips.

He stood unmoving, his lips unresponsive. She moved away and smiled sadly. "We better get moving. It will be dark soon."

They hurried across the open space toward a small cluster of trees, watchful of the sky and the rock-covered terrain.

"Do you have any water left?" Steel asked, his chest heaving and his heart thumping against his ribs from the exertion.

"Not much." Melanie handed him the canteen.

"Are you sure we'll find protection in the mountains?" he asked.

She smiled. "I'm sure, trust me."

A challenging roar from the direction of the grass-covered savannah made them both jump up. Without talking, they picked up their gear and started running for the mountain. Looking back over his shoulder, Steel spotted a head with powerful jaws above the tall grass, and then the giant dinosaur stepped out into the open.

"I hope he isn't as hungry as he sounds and looks," Steel exclaimed.

"They're always hungry. It takes a lot of meat to feed eight tons of body mass." Melanie suddenly faltered beside him.

"Give me your backpack," Steel said.

"I'm fine," she said stubbornly and stumbled again.

Steel took another glance backwards. The giant beast had ventured farther out of the tall grass, surveying the terrain. It stood on its powerful hind legs, short arms dangling, the long head with its gaping jaws moving from side to side.

Melanie stopped suddenly, bent over, gasping.

"What is it?" Steel asked, concerned.

"A cramp," she moaned. "I must have strained a muscle."

"Give me your backpack!"

He took it from her, slung it across his shoulder. "Can we stop that beast with these rifles?" he asked.

"She shook her head. "Nothing short of a cannon stops a Giganotosaurus."

"Then let's run for it." He grabbed her arm. "Come, hang on to me."

The Giganotosaurus must have spotted them. It let out a terrifying roar and began to trot in their direction.

Steel pulled Melanie with him as they staggered toward the rock she indicated. The charging behemoth had covered half the distance when they reached their destination.

"Now what?" Steel asked, looking at the sheer cliff. "No way to climb this, not without ropes," he gasped and looked back at the advancing beast, frighteningly close now. "And not enough time."

Melanie nearly ripped the backpack off his shoulder and began searching frantically inside. Pulling out a small oblong device, she pointed it at the rock wall. Staring at it, Steel noticed the thin square hairline crack in the flat surface. While he watched, a piece of rock the size of a door pushed out of the cliff and swung open to reveal an opening.

"Inside. Quick!" Melanie ordered.

Steel didn't need any encouragement. A loud roar much too close convinced him it was the best suggestion he'd heard in a long time. The door swung shut behind him, cutting off the hostile outside world. He followed Melanie down a dimly lit corridor, wondering what they would find behind the door he saw at the end of the corridor. The door was locked. Melanie pressed her hand against a metal plate in its center. As the door swung open, bright lights came to life, illuminating a room filled with humming machines and unfamiliar devices.

"What is this place?" Steel asked.

Melanie closed the door, limped over to a couch and sank into it. Patting the spot beside her, she said, "Sit down and relax. We are safe in here."

"What is this place?" he asked again.

"It's a time-terminal. A way out of here."

Before Steel could sit down, a door in the back of the room opened, and a vaguely human-looking figure walked into the room. It had no distinct features, no nose, no mouth, just a strip of opaque plastic where the eyes should have been.

"Welcome to Terminal Five, Agent Gifford." It spoke with a pleasant baritone and a peculiar accent, but Steel had no problem understanding the words.

"Bring us something to drink and eat," Melanie said.

The thing made a slight bow. "I will see to it." Then it disappeared through the door.

"An artificial life-unit," Melanie explained. "The guardian and caretaker of this terminal."

Steel sat down beside her. "I think I'm beginning to believe you," he said.

Chapter Seven

Melanie padded on bare feet across the tiled floor, stretching her muscles. "There is nothing better than a cold shower after spending the day running away from hungry dinosaurs," she said, smiling.

Steel grinned and put his arm around her naked body. "You smell a lot better now than you did before you stepped into the shower."

"So do you," she said and molded her body against his, searching for his lips. Kissing him with great passion, she let her hand travel down to his groin and giggled when her fingers curled around his hardening penis. "I thought you were tired," she said after breaking the kiss.

"Not that tired," he murmured, digging his fingers into her round buttocks.

Lifting up on tiptoes, she opened her legs a little and captured his stiff pole between her warm thighs. He moved his pelvis slowly back and forth, feeling her soft vagina lips caressing his manhood. "You feel wet," he murmured.

She laughed softly and squeezed her thighs together. "Don't explode yet; wait until you're inside me."

Picking her up, he carried her to the bed and put her down. She lay on her back, her legs wide open and smiled up at him. He studied her lovely form, the perfect breasts, the flat belly and beckoning pink cleft between her spread thighs.

"Well?" she said. "Don't let it get cold."

He joined her on the bed and lay between her legs. Then he kissed her gently. "Last night we were drunk," he said softly, "and I didn't get a chance to really enjoy your beautiful body. Let me touch every inch of you; let me feel your skin on mine. Let me love you."

Her arms went around his neck. Pulling him down on top of her, she pressed her breasts into his chest and wrapped her legs around his torso. "I've waited a long time to feel your body on mine, my love, such a long time. You have no idea. Now let me feel your hard flesh inside me, let us become one and enjoy this night, for this is all we have. We don't know what tomorrow brings."

A loud sob escaped her lips when he entered her soft moistness, and she moved against him with unexpected ferociousness. "I love you, Derek," she cried out when a climax shook her whole body. She raked her long fingers across his back and whimpered like someone in great pain. Then she relaxed and kissed him gently. "Love me, Derek," she whispered. "Please, love me, and let this moment last forever."

Steel shuddered violently as his own body was gripped by a tremendous orgasm, and holding her tight, he filled her clutching vessel with his discharge. Then they lay in each other's arms, still joined together, but unmoving.

"Promise me something," Melanie said.

"Anything," he murmured into her soft hair.

"Promise me never to forget my love for you."

He stroked her buttocks gently. "I promise."

She wiggled her bottom and squeezed him with her inner muscles. "And never forget how good it felt to be inside me." She gasped when he snapped his pelvis forward.

"Still does," he laughed, turned onto his back and pulled her on top of him. "Now *you* do all the work," he said, grinning up at her.

* * * *

"How do you manage to have fresh eggs and bread?" Steel asked her at breakfast. "And freshly ground coffee?"

"The Artificial Unit prepares it all," Melanie explained.

"But where does it come from?"

"We've had forty years to perfect traveling through time. Getting supplies from upline is not too difficult."

"Can you communicate with your people in the future?"

"Yes, I can. As a matter of fact, I'm overdue with my report."

"How long has this terminal been here?"

"About twenty years, as long as the compound. We've been monitoring the progress of the Mars-project since the beginning.

For some unexplained reason, we cannot determine when the saboteurs will strike."

He looked at her across the table. "Are you the only agent from your time on this project?"

Shaking her head, she said, "Oh, now. We have about a half dozen people observing, even working on the project. Some of them even came down from your time, after integrating themselves into your society for a number of years. I myself spent almost a year in 2182, just to learn about your way of life, before I was sent here."

"How did you become Chief of Security?" Steel asked.

Melanie smiled. "Entering a little program into your main computer is not a difficult thing to do. In fact, when I did it, I was surprised by the lack of security in your system."

"Nobody expected any saboteurs, not in the year one hundred million BC. Everyone who comes down here is screened. Now we know different. How did you get here? You weren't in my register."

"Some of the agents came through your transporter. I didn't. I arrived in this one, our own."

"Then how did you get into the compound?"

"She smiled. "As I told you before, security down here stinks. I just boarded the ship, after I ditched my personal *Jet-suit* in the jungle."

"Jet-suit?"

"I forget…you don't have those in your time." She smiled again. "One-person-propulsion devices."

"I see. How do the saboteurs get in?"

"The same way you do. You see, the years from 2065 to 2095 are critical years, and the fabric of time overlaps across many timelines. Any agent going back in time to one hundred million BC during those years will end up in the time-transporters inside your compound. I don't know why that is, I'm not a time-travel scientist. Time-agents from my time cannot get in that way. We had to build our own terminal to be able to transport people and materials back in time."

"How did you manage to build this terminal?"

40

"A small piece at a time, the same way your engineers did." Melanie looked at the timepiece on her wrist. "First, we send back a small transporter to establish a base, and then we begin sending larger components." She shrugged. "I was never really interested in the details." Again, she looked at her timepiece and then at him. Her eyes seemed suddenly filled with moisture. "I think it's time," she said, her voice faltering a little.

"Time for what?" he asked.

"Time to move on. Come with me."

He followed her into another room. Recognizing the circular platform under a transparent canopy, he said, "The transporter?"

Melanie nodded and stepped close to him. Looking into his eyes, she said, "Remember everything that happened since you arrived here. It is important. When you give your report, leave nothing out, our lives may depend on it."

Steel put a finger on her lips. "You sound so mysterious. Is this farewell?"

"For now, but don't worry, I'll be there. Now go!" She smiled bravely up at him, and then she kissed him. "I love you," she whispered and urged him onto the platform.

The last thing he remembered was her smiling face and her blue eyes, large and sad.

Then the swirling darkness took him away.

Chapter Eight

The darkness lifted, and when he looked around, momentarily disoriented, he found himself inside a strange, darkened room. The furniture looked primitive. A couch covered with cloth behind a low wooden table, a large cabinet with a computer screen in one corner, another cabinet with large buttons in the front and a cloth screen on top of another cabinet.

Seeing the curtain-covered window, he walked over to it and opened the curtains. Staring through the scratched glass, he gazed across a narrow street at the buildings on the other side. They looked strange, the designs unfamiliar. All the buildings seemed to be constructed out of bricks and stones. He remembered seeing buildings like that on old paintings. Lit-up signs above entrances and large windows advertised all kinds of establishments inside those buildings.

I know I'm in the future, but not in my time. If I remember my history correctly, I'm somewhere in the twentieth century.

He turned when he heard the opening of the door.

The woman who walked in was dressed strangely. Her blue pants were tight and rolled up. On her feet she wore white socks and black, flat shoes. She clicked something beside the door, and a light hanging from the ceiling suddenly lighted up the room. When she saw him standing by the window, her hand went up to her mouth for a split second, and then she reached into the inside of her jacket and pulled out an object he recognized.

A gun. Sleek and streamlined. Nothing that belonged to this period, of that he was certain.

"Who are you?" she asked, "and how did you get into my apartment?"

He stared into her blue eyes. She looked different. Younger somehow, her blond hair pulled back into a ponytail, but unmistakably her.

"Melanie," he called out and started walking toward her.

"Stop right there. Don't come any closer. I'm quite good with this gun. How do you know my name?"

"It's me…Derek. Don't you recognize me?"

She shook her head and motioned for him to sit down. "No. Should I?"

He looked at the weapon in her hand. "No need for that. I'm not here to harm you." He sat down and stared at her. "What year is this?"

She cocked her head. "Don't you know?"

"No, I don't. The last date I remember on my calendar said *one hundred million BC.* Does that date mean anything to you?"

"Never been there myself," she said, cautiously. "Do I look that old?"

He smiled. "No, actually you look younger than I remember."

"We know each other?" She was still watching him warily.

He nodded. "I know *you,* but it seems you don't know me…not yet. You are Melanie Gifford. When I knew you, the time you came from was the year 2145." He rubbed his forehead. "This is beginning to get quite complicated."

"You are time-traveler?" she asked.

"Yes, just like you, except we're from different times, even different timelines. I don't understand that whole concept. My present year is 2085 AD."

She seemed to relax a little, but she still eyed him with suspicion. "How did you and I meet?"

"Professionally. I'm Army-Intelligence and you are…will be Chief of Security in the year one hundred million BC at the Mars-project. We were investigating attempts to sabotage the project."

She gave him a thoughtful look. "Did you…will you find out anything?"

He shrugged. "Nothing concrete yet." He smiled grimly. "But I guess we were getting closer. Someone tried to kill us."

She smiled for the first time. "It sounds promising."

He smiled back at her, studying her. She looked the way he remembered her, close enough for him to be certain it was Melanie and not some younger look-alike. She had darkened her eyebrows and lashes and colored her lips red. But her voice was the same.

"Something wrong?" she asked, noticing his eyes on her.

He shook his head. "Nothing is wrong. Even with your face painted and your hair pulled back, you still look beautiful."

She actually blushed. "Did we have a casual relationship, or was there more to it?"

"It wasn't casual."

"We were lovers?"

"We were. Still are…in your future." He thought for a moment and chuckled. "In my past. I'm beginning to appreciate the complexities and paradoxes of traveling in time."

"It's the year 1950 AD," she said, a little smile playing around her full red lips.

"The year Mars invades Earth. In your timeline. In mine, we had a war on Earth, in a country called Korea. No Mars."

"Mars won't invade for another seven months."

"Oh." He kept looking at her. "I'm at a loss as to what to do. I'd like to take you in my arms and kiss you because I'm so happy to see you, but I don't think it would be appropriate."

"It wouldn't be. You and I are not lovers. Let's be clear about that."

"But we will be."

"Maybe. Time can change that. Nothing is certain. We might slip into another timeline." She took off her jacket and hung it on a hook beside the door. "I'm going to make something to eat. Are you hungry?"

"No, thanks. I had breakfast before I came here."

"That's hours ago."

"Not for me." He chuckled. "It was morning in one hundred million BC."

"Come with me into the kitchen so I can keep an eye on you," she said, motioning for him to go first.

The kitchen was small, consisting of a counter, a primitive cooking appliance and a round table with two chairs. Melanie opened a cabinet in one corner and took out some food. When the cool air from the open door caressed his face, he recognized the cabinet as a cooling appliance. She turned some buttons on the other appliance, and he saw a coil on its surface turn red. She put a shallow pan on it and began frying up some meat.

"Smells good," he commented.

She smiled. "Changed your mind? All I have is sausages and potatoes. Want a beer?"

"Beer?"

"An alcoholic beverage. Don't tell me you don't drink."

"I drink, alcoholic beverages, I mean. Sure, give me a beer."

When she poured him a glass and he took a sip, he felt foolish. "We don't call this beer in my time," he said, "but I'm not unfamiliar with it."

"Want a smoke?"

"A what?"

She threw a package on the table. "A cigarette."

"What do you do with it?"

"You smoke it." She pulled out a short white stick, put it into her mouth and lit it with a smaller piece of wood, which she rubbed against the side of a box to ignite. Inhaling the smoke, she blew it threw her nose.

When he waved his hand in front of his face, she laughed. "If you want to fit in, you have to learn the customs. People smoke in 1950."

"Disgusting. How long until your lungs turn black?"

She shrugged. "I agree, it's a disgusting habit and not healthy, but I'll have my lungs cleaned out when I get back to my time."

He shook his head. "You sound as if you've been here for quite some time."

"Six months," she said and stubbed out her cigarette. "I don't really have to smoke. Just wanted to test you."

"Test me?"

"You can't trust anyone, remember that. Now, tell me about you and my future self." He told her everything he remembered while she ate. From the day he arrived in the compound until the moment he stepped onto the transporter platform.

"You told me to remember every little detail. 'Leave nothing out' you said, 'our lives may depend on it'."

"You could have left out the details about our lovemaking," she said, but she smiled.

Chapter Nine

He didn't sleep well that night. The couch he lay on felt lumpy and left him with a backache in the morning. Being used to sleeping in a soundproof room, the traffic noise from the outside didn't help either.

Melanie made him a breakfast of bacon and eggs and coffee.

"These chickens are probably running around free on some farm," she smiled when he looked at the red yolk. "I have a friend who has connections to a farmer. The eggs are cheaper that way."

"Cheaper? I don't understand. Aren't all commodities controlled by the government?"

"Not in 1950. Things are a little different here. They use a system called *Free Enterprise*. You pay for things with money made from paper and metal."

"They don't use chips?"

She shook her head. "No computers. They haven't been invented yet." She chuckled. "Chips are something you eat."

"How can people function without computers? Must be terribly complicated."

"Just the opposite. Everything seems much simpler than in my time, and in yours, I'm sure." She sighed. "Maybe even better. There are fewer people, and they seem to be more carefree and happier."

"Let me ask you a question, Melanie. Why are you here in this particular time?"

"I'm here to make certain the invasion happens," she said.

"How can you do that?"

"Let me show you something." She got up, went over to a cabinet and took something out of it. "This is yesterday's newspaper. Read it."

He picked up the large sheet of paper. "They print the news on actual paper?" he asked, his voice sounding surprised.

"They have audio reports on radios and visual reports on television." She pointed to the glass screen in the large cabinet.

"I thought that was a primitive computer."

"I told you, computers haven't been invented yet."

He looked at the paper and the date. February 10, 1950. The headline screamed in bold letters:

MARS INVASION IMMINENT!

In a speech before a Republican women's group in Wheeling, West Virginia, yesterday, Senator McCarthy accused the State Department of harboring traitorous Martians. He claims that Secretary of State, Dean Acheson, knows of at least two hundred and five Martians in the State Department. He is calling for an investigation and urges the US government to build more aircraft and increase the number of men in the Air Force and prepare planet Earth against an invasion from our neighboring planet, Mars. Furthermore, he criticized President Truman's foreign policy agenda.

Reports of UFO sightings all across the United States are becoming a daily occurrence.

Folding the paper, Steel said, "I'm not a history buff, but I'm sure that in my…timeline this never happened."

Melanie nodded. "You are correct, it never did. I know this, because I've been to your timeline, or one close to it. In the year 1950. I saw the same headline. However, McCarthy wasn't worried about Martians. He accused the State of harboring Communists."

"Communists?"

"Members who belong to a party that believes individuals don't own property, it belongs to everybody. Communism was a great threat to the free world. It exists here, too, but none of it won't matter in a few months when Mars invades Earth."

"If it is going to happen why do you have to be here? I don't understand."

"We visited other timelines and found a few where the US government listened to McCarthy and built up its Armed Forces. When the Martians landed, they met resistance, and in some timelines, the Martian invading force was defeated. In some, atomic bombs were deployed and the Earth destroyed in 1950." She stared at him across the table, her blue eyes blazing. "Now do you understand why the Mars Invasion has to be successful?"

She looked so passionate and beautiful as she stared at him, he wanted to get up, take her into his arms and kiss her red lips, but he controlled himself. *We are strangers. She won't be the woman I love for a number of years.* Another thought suddenly struck him. She had known him when he arrived in the compound in one hundred million BC, and she couldn't tell him that. In some ways, she must have felt the same way he felt now.

"Why are you staring at me like that?" Her voice interrupted his thoughts.

"Sorry," he apologized. "I wasn't aware I was staring," he said with a disarming smile.

"You were."

"Don't mean to. It is just so hard for me to forget about my relationship with your older version."

"Well...forget it! Pretend you and I are strangers, which is true for me." She finished her cup of coffee and lit up a cigarette. When he gave her a disgusted look, she shrugged. "You make me feel uncomfortable. Smoking calms my nerves."

"It irritates my throat," he said. "Why do I make you feel uncomfortable?"

"I don't know. You just do. I don't know what to do with you. Why has my future self sent you here?"

"She must have had her reasons. Maybe to let you know everything is going to be all right."

"Maybe, but as I said before, nothing is certain. Anything can go wrong. Somebody meddles with the wrong events and reality takes a different direction, slips into another shadow-timeline."

Her words sounded grave and made him shiver.

"Perhaps we're interfering with something we shouldn't," he said.

"You may be right. Humanity is playing God. Who knows what damage we will manage to inflict on the fabric of the universe by changing history. Only time will tell." She smiled at her own pun.

"To come back to my earlier question. What do you have to do to make the invasion successful?"

She blew a few smoke rings out of rounded red lips and watched them grow larger until they dissipated. Then she gave him a long look. "We have to discredit Senator McCarthy. We must make him look like a lunatic who has lost his objective."

"How?"

"By feeding rumors to the right people. By denying that Mars is even populated. So far, the only thing Earth people have seen are UFO's. Unidentified Flying Objects. Even the government is trying hard to deny their existence. There is no proof yet that Martians exist. Astronomers see only a green planet from Earth."

"I thought Mars is red."

"Maybe in your timeline, not in this one. Not after the successful terra-forming." She stumped out her cigarette in a glass dish and got up. "Time to talk to some people. You might as well come along, as my protector."

When he raised an eyebrow, she said, "Some of the people I'm dealing with are rough. They see women as objects, better suited for a bedroom instead of a boardroom."

Chapter Ten

Gray clouds obscured the sky, and a slight drizzle put a chill into the air. Steel pulled the collar of his black uniform jacket closer around his neck and looked at the strange vehicle Melanie had parked in the back lane. Red in color, with a split windshield and a sun visor, it looked heavy and cumbersome.

Sliding into the passenger seat, he turned his head to look out of the small rear window. Melanie chuckled when she took her seat behind a wheel, which he assumed was used to turn the big tires underneath the vehicle. She inserted a key into a slot and turned it. The motor sprang to life with a loud roar.

"1948 Chevy Coupe," she said. "Six cylinders. Plenty of power."

"These vehicles don't ride on aircushions?" he asked.

"No, they roll on tires, and they use gasoline to power the engine." She moved a stick between their seats and pushed her foot against a lever on the floor. The vehicle began to move, slowly at first, but accelerated as Melanie applied more pressure to the lever.

"Gasoline," he said, "a highly inflammable liquid used in internal-combustion engines, which produce loud noises and emit a toxic gas known as carbon monoxide. I know the principle. Are you sure this thing is safe?"

She laughed. "As safe as the driver. Don't worry, I've been driving this car long enough, and I can handle it."

They came out of the back lane and joined the traffic on the street.

"I'm surprised people could stand the noise and the smell without getting sick," Steel said. "I already feel nauseated, and I thought one hundred million BC was bad."

"You'll get used to it." Melanie accelerated, changed lanes and passed the car in front of them. "Sunday driver!" she cursed, giving Steel cause to glance at her.

"There are no seatbelts to secure yourself," he commented.

"You want me to burn rubber?" Melanie asked, laughing.

"What? Why would you burn rubber?"

"An expression. It means to accelerate fast." She shrugged. "Before I came here, I had to learn the 1950's slang. It's important to fit in. That can sometimes be the hardest part, especially at times like these, when anyone who stands out is accused of being a traitor." She gave him a quick glance. "You know, we'll have to get some different clothes for you. In that outfit, you *do* look like someone from another planet."

With a curse, she slammed her foot on the brakes and then accelerated again. "Shit!" she exclaimed. "Just went through a red light, and the *Heat* is right behind us."

"The *Heat*?"

"Cops. The police. Dammit!"

Before Steel even heard a siren blaring outside, Melanie pulled over to the side. "Let me do the talking," she advised him. "The less visible you are, the better it will be."

Rolling down the window on her side, Melanie smiled up at the uniformed policeman, rapping something alongside the car. "Good morning, officer."

"Are you aware that you just ran a red light, sister?"

"I am, and I am sorry. My foot must have got stuck on the petal."

"I'll say. You laid a patch on the road so long they'll have to bring in a special crew to clean up this mess." His gaze fell on Steel. "Who's the guy in the funny threads?"

"He's... my fiancé."

"Fiancé? Why's he dressed like that? You a Martian?" He glared at Steel.

"A Martian?" Melanie laughed. "You're a big tickle, officer."

"Cut the gas! I wasn't talking to you, sister."

"You surely don't believe in Martians, sir?" Steel gave the policeman a friendly smile. "I've just auditioned for a play. I'm an actor."

"You have a funny way of talking. Show me some papers."

Steel shrugged. "Can't do that. I lost them."

"He's Canadian," Melanie said. "They talk funny."

The policeman twisted around and called to someone in the

police car. "Hey, Marty, get on the horn and tell them we're bringing in a couple of suspects." Then he turned back to Melanie. "Step out of the car...and you, too, mister. Hands reaching."

Steel looked at Melanie. She just shrugged. "Better do what he says. I don't feel like getting burned."

Steel opened the car door and stepped onto the pavement. He heard Melanie do the same. When the policeman grabbed Melanie's arm and pushed her against the car, he said harshly, "Hey, no need for rough stuff. She's hasn't done anything."

"She ran a red light, so don't rattle your cage!" The policeman ran his hands down Melanie's body, touching her a little bit too long for Steel's taste. "What do we have here?" he said triumphantly, pulling the gun out of her jacket pocket.

"It's a prop-gun," Melanie said. "My fiancé auditioned for a Science Fiction movie called *Invasion from Mars*." She smiled at him. "Dig it, Daddy-O? Invasion from Mars. Doesn't that sound like a blast?" She wiggled her hips. "Now...why don't we just forget this whole thing. Call it a misunderstanding. What do you say?" Her hand went up to open a button on her blouse.

He stared at her open jacket, at the deep cleavage suddenly so visible to his view.

"Come one, don't be a wet rag, officer." Her smile could have melted an iceberg.

The policeman's face softened a little. His hand cupped her breast, squeezed it. "You're surely stacked well," he murmured. Pulling his hand away, he said, "Don't let me catch you again, all right doll?" With that, he walked away, back to his car.

Steel got into the car, breathing a sigh of relief. "What kind of language was that?" he asked Melanie when she slipped into her seat. "I understood only half of it. Is that the way they talk here?"

She gave him a mischievous chuckle. "Not exactly. I might have overplayed it a little. But it worked. I'm actually a good judge of character."

"The way he fondled you. I was ready to start a fight," he said, more angrily than he intended.

"You're sweet," she said. "I'm glad you didn't, though."

"You know, this may come out of the blue, but I just remembered something. Melanie...you in the future...told me to remember the name Miles Tyde. I didn't know why it was important, but I have a feeling it is."

"Miles Tyde?" Melanie repeated the name. "She...I...must have meant Senator Miles Tyde. This is strange. Senator Tyde is giving a political speech tonight at a fundraiser in the Rotary Club. I had in mind to talk to him, but somehow I didn't think he could to anything. You see, in your timeline, the U.S. government had McCarthy investigated by a Senate panel, which uncovered unethical behavior in McCarthy's tax returns and in his campaigns. It didn't actually happen until 1952, but this is a different timeline with different circumstances."

Her eyes studied Steel. "I have a feeling the reason you are here is to steer me in the right direction. I...in the future, know the outcome of this." She smiled broadly. "I believe we'll be successful."

"I like your enthusiasm," Steel cautioned, "but you don't even know the man. How will you get close to him and make him listen to you?"

"You forget I've been here for months. I did make some connections. Joe Marianzo is one of them. He'll get me into the club."

"Who's Joe Marianzo?"

"He is the head of the local mob, also a good friend to the Mayor."

"Wonderful!" Steel exclaimed. "Now we're getting involved with the underworld. What circles are you running in?"

"The one that can help with our quest. After the invasion, anyone plotting against the new masters is a criminal." Melanie pulled the car into the traffic. "But first, we have to get you properly dressed."

* * * *

"Glad to be of help, doll." Joe Marianzo shifted his great bulk and smiled jovially at Melanie. "I made a lot of money, legally, with that tip you gave me. Those stocks are going through the roof." He gave Steel a sharp look. "She's a good kid, almost like my own sister. You take good care of her."

"I will," Steel said, with a glance at Melanie. "I love her very much. Thanks for the reference. I'll get your friend to make me a new set of identification papers."

"You talk funny," Marianzo said. "Better practice your accent. You've got *foreigner* written all over you."

"He's from Canada," Melanie said.

"Maybe he is, maybe he isn't." Marianzo's little pig's eyes squinted at her. "It makes no difference to me where he's from, and I don't care what he's done. I'm in the business myself, and I know sometimes one has to change his identity." He sighed and took a sip from a glass. "I won't be at the club tonight. These political speeches bore me. When you get to the door, ask for Frankie Malone. He'll get you a couple of press passes."

"Thanks, Godfather." Melanie bent over the table and gave him a good look at her breasts. "I won't forget this."

"I know you won't." Marianzo winked at her. "Maybe some day, when my wife isn't home, you come to my house for a drink."

"Maybe." Melanie smiled and fluttered her eyelids.

When they were outside, Steel threw a disapproving look at her. "Like his own sister, huh? Is there something going on between you and that mountain of blubber?"

"What do you mean?"

"The way you acted in there. Embarrassing."

Her laughter was genuine. It didn't help his mood. "Are you jealous? If you are, you have no reason to be. You and I, we are not lovers."

Sighing, he got into the car. "Let's go and get my forged papers. I hope that guy he's sending us to is as good as he says."

"He is," Melanie assured him. "He made mine."

* * * *

Senator Tyde waved his hand impatiently when Melanie approached him. "Speak with my aid. I don't have time to talk to reporters right now."

"I'm not really a reporter," Melanie said, "and it is important I talk with you."

He gave her a curious glance. "If you're not a reporter, why are you wearing a press pass?"

She smiled disarmingly. "It was the only way to get in here."

"Who are you, and what do you want?"

"I want to talk to you about Senator McCarthy."

That seemed to catch his attention. "What about McCarthy?"

She looked around the room, noticing some of the other guests sitting at the tables throwing curious glances in their direction. "Not here. Too many listeners. Can we talk somewhere more private?"

The Senator seemed to take notice of Steel for the first time. "Are you with her?"

Steel nodded but didn't say anything.

"My colleague," Melanie said. "We are members of a think tank, and we have valuable information you should have."

"Okay," Tyde said. "We can go to my hotel room." He waved to a couple of burly men, who had been watching, and then he started walking toward the exit, accompanied by Steel and Melanie. When Steel looked back, he saw the two men following them.

They took an elevator up two floors and then walked down a short corridor to the Senator's suit. The two guards stepped out of another elevator. Another guard stood outside the door, eyeing them with suspicion as they approached.

"You certainly believe in security," Steel commented.

"One can't be too careful these days," the Senator said and stopped in front of his door. He nodded to the guard. "Is Cindy in?"

"She is," the guard said and stepped aside. Tyde knocked on the door, and a few moments later, it opened to reveal an older woman, dressed in a gray business suit.

"This is Cindy, my private secretary," Tyde said. "She'll write down everything you'll tell me." He walked over to a chair and flopped into it. "I'll give you twenty minutes. I'm quite tired."

Melanie and Steel took seats across from him. "We have reason to believe that Senator McCarthy is cheating on his taxes,"

Melanie started.

"I'm listening."

"However, that is not what we're here to tell you. Others have already made those allegations. We've done an analysis of his policy. If he convinces the State Department to increase the size of our military forces, it will lead to a costly war with the USSR within five years. If both sides deploy atomic weapons, and the chances for that happening are seventy percent correct, much of the United States will be destroyed and millions of lives lost."

"How do you know this?" The Senator looked skeptical.

"As I told you, we are members of a think tank, and that's what we do. Our predictions have a sixty-three percent certainty of being accurate."

The Senator crossed his legs and leaned forward. "Tell me more."

Chapter Eleven

"Pretty clever and ingenious." Steel studied the round metal platform the area rug had concealed. Looking up at the ceiling, he said, "I thought that thing up there was some artistic design."

Melanie laughed cheerfully. "That's what it's supposed to look like."

"I wondered how I ended up in your living room. I didn't see a time-transporter. Where are the controls?"

She pointed to the cabinet that held the TV. "In there. Behind a false wall."

"Is the transporter alive? Can you transport yourself out of here at any time?"

She shook her head. "No. That's why I was so surprised to see you. I'm not expecting anyone for another four months."

"Why is that?"

"It has something to do with time-paradox. I don't really know."

"How about me? Am I stuck here with you?" Pulling the piece of carpet back over the metal plate, he gave her a questioning look. After being in this place for over a month now, he began to wonder what was going to happen to him if the Mars-project proved successful. Would he cease to exist? Would he have to stay in the year 1950 in a timeline that wasn't his own? Could he ever get back to 2085? Questions he had pondered for days now.

"I can't give you an answer," Melanie said. "I wish I could."

"I'm itching for some action," Steel said. "Sitting around like this and waiting for I don't know what is driving me crazy."

"How about a movie?" Melanie asked. A drive-in movie. I've never been to one."

"Neither have I." Steel shrugged. "All right. Maybe it'll cheer me up."

"Wonderful!" Melanie seemed exited about going to watch a movie projected onto a giant flat screen, which they had to watch from inside a car. Somehow, Steel couldn't share her enthusiasm, but he was willing to humor her.

They drove almost half an hour to get to the drive-in theatre. Plenty of cars lined up already, but they managed to find a good spot. The night was chilly, but a small electric heater provided adequate warmth. The sound came from a speaker, which they hung on one of the side-windows.

Before the main feature began, they watched news reports from around the world and then a short animated film. Steel admitted grudgingly the antics of the drawn animal characters did make him laugh.

By the time the feature film with the title *The Loves of Carmen* started, Steel felt relaxed enough to enjoy the popcorn Melanie offered him.

He reminded himself that things were different in 1950. Three-dimensional images didn't exist. Interactive performances were something nobody even dreamed of. The outcome of a movie always seemed the same. It never changed. The sound was terrible, tinny and flat, and the images on the screen without any dimensions, but he was willing to enjoy it all.

He learned a lot about this period these last few weeks. People acted prudish, in real life and on the screen. Nudity in public was not tolerated, offenders arrested and charged with indecent exposure. Sex was not something discussed in public or seen on the screen.

He watched the movie with more interest than desire to be entertained, but after awhile, he did enjoy the story, even though the acting seemed stilted and unnatural, the monologue unreal sometimes. When he looked at Melanie and saw her dabbing her eyes with a handkerchief, he asked, "Are you crying?"

"Shh…" she whispered. "Don't spoil it."

She seemed to have edged closer, and following an impulse, he put his arm around her shoulder. She snuggled up against him, and suddenly she grabbed his head and kissed him. Surprised by her action, he was slow to respond, but then he returned her kiss with great passion.

When they broke apart, he said, "This comes a little unexpected. I'm at a loss as to how to react."

"Isn't that what you've always wanted?" she whispered.

"Ever since I arrived." He bent to kiss her again.

She clung to him like a drowning victim to a rescuer. "I've been so lonely from the first day I came here. Things are so different. People are different. They have such hang-ups and so many taboos. I can't become too attached to anyone, can't speak freely with the people I associate with. The greatest burden is the responsibility I carry. How can I all by myself make it an absolute certainty a war that will cost a billion lives will happen?"

He looked into her face, saw the brave smile and the tears streaming down her cheeks. Wiping them off with his finger, he said gently, "You're not alone, not anymore."

"I'm so glad you're here," she said. "Let's go home."

"But the film hasn't ended yet," he protested.

She smiled. "I've seen it before. I know the ending. Let's go, before I change my mind."

They drove home in silence. The moment they entered their apartment, Melanie was in his arms and covered his face with wet kisses. Then she pulled him into the bedroom. "Give me a minute," she whispered and rushed into the bathroom.

When she came back out, she was naked. He sat at the edge of the bed and watched her walking toward him, all soft and curvy, the weak glow from the light bulb throwing parts of her body into mysterious shadow.

"Why are you still dressed?" she asked, puzzled, and put an arm across her breasts, suddenly bashful.

"I didn't know what to expect," he said slowly.

She walked up to him and put her breasts against his face. He inhaled her fragrance, so familiar and so different, and pressed his face into her deep cleavage. Looking up into her smiling face, he said, "I've missed you."

"I'm here now," she said huskily and sat in his lap. With deft fingers, she began unbuttoning his shirt. "I feel cold," she pouted. "I need a warm body against mine."

"Then let me get undressed." He chuckled and pushed her off.

"I'll help you. You're too slow. I could freeze to death before you're naked." She giggled and opened his belt. Then she pushed down his pants and exposed his erection. Sinking to the floor in front of him, she licked her lips. "He's big," she murmured and put her tongue on the tip of his member.

He groaned when he felt her feathery touch and put his hands against her head. Her lips opened, and slowly she took him into her mouth. Closing his eyes, he enjoyed her gentle tonguing.

She freed him before he came too close to climaxing and looked up at him, blue eyes veiled behind lowered long lashes. "You like that?" she asked and slid her tongue up his belly and his chest. Her lips touched his, and when her teeth pressed against his teeth, he let her in.

She pushed against him and made him sit at the edge of the bed. Turning around, she presented her lovely buttocks and sat in his lap. His stiff penis slid between her soft thighs. She moved slowly up and down, rubbing her clit along the length of his rigid shaft. Her hand reached between her thighs and taking his scrotum into her hand, she squeezed it gently.

Suddenly she moaned loudly, with swift movements she lifted higher, and then he felt his mast sliding into hot moistness.

"This feels good," she groaned and gyrated her pelvis in his lap.

He reached around her to cup her ample breasts. Taking her nipples between his fingers, he rolled them until they became hard and solid, like a couple of tiny penises. She let out a sobbing cry and sat quivering in his lap, her inner muscles working feverishly. He felt her warm discharge running down between his thighs.

Sliding from his lap, she knelt on the floor and pushed up her rump. He positioned himself behind her and stroked her sleek arched back and lovely shaped buttocks. "You haven't changed at all," he murmured, forgetting for the moment that this was Melanie's younger self.

She wriggled her bottom. "I'm getting cold down there, Derek."

This was the first time she had called him by his first name, and it sounded good to his ears.

She smiled and moved forward, putting his rigid organ between her lovely cheeks. Her hand reached between her legs, grabbed his penis firmly and guided him. Pushing backwards, she sheathed his penis inside her soft and wet pussy.

He grabbed her hips and began to slide in and out of her with forceful thrusts. She whimpered and clawed at the carpet when an orgasm shook her body. Her hair, now loose, swirled around her head as she threw it from side to side. "You're killing me, Derek," she sobbed, "but don't stop."

Trying to steady her bucking body, Steel almost slipped out of her, but he managed to hold on to her rotating pelvis.

"You can come inside me," she whispered after she calmed down. "I'm protected."

"You're sure?"

"I'm sure. Let me feel your essence shoot into me, my love. I want to feel you come."

As if on cue, he felt the sweet heavenly pleasure rushing up and let it consume him. With a loud shout, he pushed deep into her, clamped his hands around her hips and released his sperm. Melanie milked him with enthusiasm. Crying something in another language, she quivered in his grip as if experiencing an electric shook and doused him with so much warm liquid, he became afraid she'd ruptured something inside her.

Collapsing on top of her, he lay like that for a long time, trying to still his ragged breathing. Underneath him, Melanie's breath came in great gasps. After a while, she stirred and clenched her buttocks, squeezing his limp penis between them.

"I guess I exhausted him," she murmured.

He chuckled into her disheveled hair. "It seems so, but he recuperates fast. We can do this again tomorrow night."

She laughed softly. "Aren't we taking things for granted, just a little bit too soon?"

When he slipped off her, she turned and wrapped her arms around him. "I don't ever want you to leave me, my love." She sighed deeply. "At least, not for a little while."

Chapter Twelve

According to newspaper articles and news reports on the radio and on television, not many people took Senator McCarthy's allegations seriously. The Senate refused to listen to his tirades about the Martians and instead of spending more money on the military, it was decided to decrease the size of the military forces.

"I've been here four months now," Steel said to Melanie. "When exactly is this invasion supposed to take place?"

"Not for another three months," Melanie said, putting the newspaper on the table. "Looks like Senator Tyde's investigation into Senator McCarthy's affairs is having the desired effect. Most people think he's a fool, and his popularity at the polls has dropped."

Steel joined her on the couch and put an arm around her. "I can't believe it's been three months since I made love to you for the first time." He grinned. "I mean to you, as you are now, not the Melanie of the future."

She laid her head against his shoulder and chuckled. "It's a good thing I've had my preventative shots, otherwise I'd be pregnant for sure by now. Have we missed one night without making love?"

"Let's see," he said, ticking off his fingers. "There was last night, the night before, and the night before that, no, that was Sunday. We had sex in the morning and in the evening." Grinning, he shook his head. "My memory is not that good. I think loosing all my sperm night after night is draining my brain cells."

"Oh, you," she chided and slapped him playfully. Offering her lips, she said, "Come, kiss me."

He kissed her gently, savoring the softness of her lips and the fragrance of her body. When he put his hand on her breast, it didn't take long for her breathing to quicken and her kisses to become more demanding. "It's not Sunday," she whispered, when he began to unbutton her blouse.

"I know, but we can pretend." He kissed her exposed breast and laughed when she squirmed in his arms.

"I…" She didn't finish her sentence.

A loud beeping sound made them both jump up. Quickly buttoning up her blouse, Melanie said, "The time-transporter. Someone is coming through."

Steel watched the air thicken and shimmer in the space between the hidden metal plate and the contraption on the ceiling. A shadow formed, took on the shape of a human body, and then a man in a shiny uniform stepped off the plate and looked around. When he spotted them, he raised a hand in greeting. "Melanie Gifford?" he asked.

"That's me."

The man looked at Steel. "Are you ready to travel, Mr. Steel?"

"Travel where?"

"Across the timelines." The man smiled thinly. "It's time for you to move on."

"When?"

"Now."

"So suddenly?" Steel turned to Melanie who stood silently with her arms hanging by her sides. He saw the tears streaming down her face. "I knew this day had to come," she whispered, smiling sadly. "That's why I tried to give you as much of myself as I could in the short time we had together." Stepping close to him, she looked into his eyes. "Good bye, my love, until we meet again." She put her arms around him and kissed him.

Her tears wet his face. Holding her tight, he suppressed a sob that tried to escape his lips. She would see him again, but would he?

Letting go of her, he stepped back and looked down at himself. "I don't think I can travel in these clothes. I'd like my own back."

Melanie went into the bedroom and recovered his clothing. When Steel dressed, he nodded to the man in the shiny uniform, who waited patiently. "I'm ready."

Standing on the metal plate, he looked back at Melanie with a sudden sense of déjà vu.

Her large blue eyes watched him with great sadness. She lifted a hand and blew him a kiss. Her whispered words *I love yo*u were the last sound he heard.

Chapter Thirteen

Traveling across time was not instantaneous. He floated in a gray mist, a rushing sound, like that of a great storm in the distance, assaulted not only his ears but all his senses. Light and darkness flickered alternately across his eyes. Images formed and dissolved, almost clear one moment and grotesquely distorted the next. It didn't matter if he kept his eyes open or closed.

Suddenly, the darkness lifted, and the storm subsided.

He stood inside a circular room, on a flat shiny plate.

"We've arrived," said a male voice beside him. "Please step off the transporter. I have to move on."

Steel had almost forgotten about his companion. Without further thought, he followed the man's orders. When he looked back, the platform was empty.

He didn't see any windows. Cold light from the ceiling lit up the room, without throwing any shadows. Looking around, he noticed a door on one end and a huge mirror on one of the walls. Probably one way, he thought.

Wondering what to do next, he walked toward the door, but before he reached it, it swung open.

He stared at the figure standing in the doorway.

"Hello, Derek," she said, and then she was in his arms, covering his face with kisses.

"Melanie," was all he could say.

When they finally broke apart, she stepped back and looked at him. "Miss me?" she asked, a mischievous smile on her face.

He grinned. "In a way I did, and in a way I didn't. But you know that already."

"How is my younger self?" she asked.

"She was fine when I left her, but you know that also. How long for you until we met in the year one hundred million BC?"

"Four years." She sighed. "A long time. An eternity."

"And this time?"

"For me? Only two weeks." She slipped back into his arms and looked up at him. "You know, this may sound foolish, but when I sent you ahead to meet my younger self, I was jealous of her. Even knowing it was me, it seemed I was sending you into the arms of another woman. But it needed to be done. Otherwise, we may never have met."

"Somehow, I can't quite figure out this whole sequence," Steel said. "Where and when are we now?"

"It's 2085 in a timeline very close to yours. Reality has already shifted; your own timeline is a shadow-line now. So is mine. We still have work to do." She pulled his face close to hers and kissed him on the lips. "I'm so happy to see you, my love. I didn't know if I would ever see you again, or how long we'd be apart."

"Over four months for me," he said.

Her blue eyes stared into his, and her lips pouted. "Don't complain. I know what you did during the last three."

"What *we* did," he corrected her.

"You're right. *We*."

"Why are we here?" Steel asked. "What happened after you sent me to 1950?"

"After you left, I transported upline to 2146, where I went through a debriefing and where I brushed up on new developments. As to why we are here? Simple. We'll have to acquire a power pack and spare components for the rover, go back and repair it, and then we'll travel to Station Alpha."

"Won't they ask questions?"

"They will, and we'll tell them our rover broke down, but we managed to repair it."

"What about the saboteurs?"

Melanie chuckled. "You worry too much, Derek. They'll wonder, but they won't ask us any questions."

When they walked through the door into the adjacent room, Steel was surprised to find himself in an office. Men and women sat behind desks and computers, doing whatever jobs they had been assigned.

"Our headquarters in 2085," Melanie explained. "We've been in this building for five years now."

Steel noticed that she didn't wear her uniform but clothing

that was in style in the 2080s. He looked down at himself, at his own uniform. "I think I should change into suitable attire before I venture outside."

"We can't chance it that someone sees and recognizes you. After all, you're supposed to be in one hundred million BC. You'll have to stay here while I get the components."

"How about someone recognizing you?" Steel asked.

"I'll wear a wig," she said. "Don't worry, I don't have too many friends in 2085. Besides, someone else will do the buying. I'll only go along to make sure we get the right stuff."

Nobody paid them any attention when they walked through the office. Melanie took him down a corridor and into another room. It had a couch, a few chairs and a small table.

"I'll have someone bring you something to drink and some food," she said. "I'll be back soon." She chuckled. "Enjoy the luxuries of the twenty-first century, for tonight you'll be going back to one hundred million BC, back when dinosaurs were kings." She pointed to a small console on the table. "There is a holo-projector. Lose yourself in a world of fantasy for a couple of hours. I know you haven't enjoyed any decent entertainment for the last four months."

"I've had plenty," he said, and grinned. "Every night...or don't you remember?"

"I remember," she said softly and left.

Chapter Fourteen

It felt strange to be back. The farther they floated away from the temporal transporter in the cliff, the quicker the events of the last four months became nothing but memories. The image of the Megalosaurus chasing them seemed fresher in his mind than the time he spent in 1950.

He glanced at Melanie who flew beside him and then at the three men slightly above them, huge rifles in their hands, ready to blast anything that might challenge their presence here. Another man, the technician, made up the rear. Steel knew that even he carried a weapon.

These people weren't taking any chances.

Once a flock of giant-winged reptiles crossed their path, but otherwise their flight across the savannah passed without any incidents. They made the trip, which had taken him and Melanie a few hours, in less than an hour with their personal jet-suits.

Their damaged rover lay where they left it. Steel expected a rusted wreck, but then he reminded himself only four days had passed in one hundred million BC since they walked away from it to find shelter in the mountains.

There wasn't much left of the dead reptile that had attacked them, except for a giant pile of bones.

The three men with the big rifles stood guard while the technician exchanged the damaged parts in the rover. The little man worked silently, except for the occasional complaint about the heat and the humidity. "I bet you could fry eggs on the rocks," he commented. "And these damned insects. Can't wait to get backs to civilization."

After about thirty minutes, he wiped his forehead and nodded to Melanie. "It should work now. Give it a try," he said, packing away his tools.

Melanie slid into the rover, and moments later the motor sprang silently to life. Lights flashed for a few seconds, and then a barely audible humming testified that the motor worked again.

Steel and Melanie rolled up their jet-suits and handed the

small packages to the technician. He stuffed them into his backpack and smiled at Melanie. "Good luck," he said and pointed toward the river. "You better hurry to get away from this hospitable place. Guests are coming, and they look hungry."

Steel followed his gaze and saw a number of dark backs appearing out of the murky surface. "Thanks for your help," he said to the technician.

They watched the four men take off, and then they sealed themselves into the rover. Melanie touched Steel's hand. "It seems we never left, doesn't it?"

He chuckled and leaned over to kiss her. "I'm glad to be back. This traveling through time is as confusing as Hell."

She laughed. "I've never been to Hell. I heard it's hot there."

"Then we're in Hell now," Steel said. "According to this gauge it's forty-five degrees Celsius out there. Lucky we have air-conditioning."

Melanie glanced out of the window. "I guess we better leave. These guys look much too curious."

Lifting into the sky, Melanie skimmed the tall grass back toward Station Zeta.

Chapter Fifteen

Melanie decided to fly directly to Station Alpha and not bother stopping at Station Zeta. She also decided to fly along the coast, a longer trip but safer than traveling down the river.

The technician had not repaired the rocket-launcher on top of the rover, since it was bent too much and he didn't have the tools required to straighten out the mount and the swivel. It didn't matter because they had no plans to land anywhere and didn't really have to worry about being attacked by flying reptiles.

The sun began to dip toward the horizon, and its glittering rays turned the waves of the ocean into a sparkling field of rolling colors.

"Isn't it beautiful?" Melanie asked.

"It is," Steel agreed, "but I can't see a damned thing against that glare."

Melanie manually darkened the windshield a little more. "There, is that better?"

"I guess." He laughed suddenly. "Funny, how quickly we adapt to conditions. A few days ago, I lived in a time where there was no air-conditioning in the vehicles called cars. They were noisy and smelly, and they didn't have windows that could be darkened to keep out the glare of sun. Surprisingly, I was actually quite happy there."

"Is it possible the fact I was there could have had something to do with it?" Melanie asked, smiling.

"Possibly." He grinned and leaned back into his seat. "But I feel quite happy and comfortable right now."

"That's because…" She stopped in mid-sentence. "Dammit! Something is wrong. We seem to be losing power."

The rover began dropping lower, and then it touched down and came to a halt.

"How far is it to Station Alpha?" Steel asked.

"Too far to walk, if that's what you mean."

"Shit! What now?"

"Maybe we can fix it." Melanie opened the door. Hot, humid

air and the sound of the nearby surf entered the cabin.

"Be careful," Steel warned. He reached behind the seat for one of the rifles.

Melanie removed the panel that covered the motor and stared at the exposed components. Putting her face close to it, she sniffed. "I don't smell anything burning. That's a good sign. Everything looks fine to me."

Steel stared at the waves rolling against the rocky shore, wondering what kind of creatures lived in the ocean. Nothing small, he felt sure of that. Then he gazed at the nearby jungle and at the bleak strip of rock-covered beach between the ocean and the jungle. Even if the safety of the compound were close, he didn't have much hope of reaching it alive. Especially traveling at night. If they couldn't get the rover mobile, the best thing they could do was to settle in for the night, inside the vehicle. Then in the morning, someone could come pick them up, providing they could contact Station Alpha. Assuming the comm still worked. Somehow, Steel had a bad feeling about that.

"Maybe they sold us faulty stuff," he said to Melanie, who still stared at the silent motor, as if she could bring it back to life by just looking at it.

"The technician checked it all out. He would have discovered any damaged components." She shook her head. "This is a mystery."

Steel didn't know what made him turn his head, but when he did, what he saw gave him an uneasy sensation in his belly. Melanie looked at the same time as he did.

About a hundred feet away floated a large disk. The rays of the evening sun bathed it with silvery red brilliance. It hung motionless in the air.

"What the hell is that?" Steel glanced at Melanie. "One of yours?"

"No. We have nothing like that. It shouldn't be here. Not in one hundred million BC."

The disk descended slowly and settled onto the ground. An opening appeared in its side, and a tell figure jumped out.

The sun was at the stranger's back, making it difficult to

determine if it was a man or a woman, but whoever came walking toward them was definitely humanoid.

Steel became aware of the rifle in his hand. He did not intend to make any threatening moves, but he kept his finger on the trigger. He waited until their visitor stopped in front of them, and then he said, "Whoever you are, I hope you came to help us get out of here."

The stranger lifted a hand. "Please, put down you weapon, before you accidentally shoot someone, Derek Steel. I mean you no harm." The voice sounded deep and resonant. A man's voice.

"How do you know my name?" Steel asked, perplexed. "Who are you?"

"Who I am is not important." The stranger smiled. "I know everything about you and," turning to Melanie, "you, Melanie Gifford."

Steel studied the man. He wore a tight, silvery uniform that accented his muscular frame. His handsome face looked tanned under his short-cropped blond hair. Steel also noticed the bright blue color of his eyes.

The man made a motion with his hand. Suddenly, behind him, appeared what could only be described as a metal chair. A being, not wholly human but human-like, sat in the chair. Tiny, bluish-green scales covered the humanoid face. Black eyes glowed darkly under thick ridges above a long slit, where the nose should have been.

When the creature opened its wide mouth, Steel could see tiny white teeth behind its human lips. A long, split tongue appeared for a quick moment, and then the creature spoke. "The Gifford and the Steel must live. It is of great importance."

Melanie tilted her head and asked, "Why wouldn't we live?"

"If you are allowed to enter Station Alpha, you will not live," said the man.

"Why not?"

"Because your vehicle contains a bomb which is set to explode once inside the compound. It will destroy the time-transporter and the seeding of planet Mars will fail. The fabric of time will be damaged and they," he pointed a finger at the creature in the chair, "will cease to exist."

"Who put this bomb into our rover?"

"The technician who repaired your vehicle. He was a spy."

"I can hardly believe that. All our people are investigated thoroughly," Melanie protested.

The man smiled thinly. "Obviously not as thoroughly as you believe."

"How do you know all this? Who are you?"

"We are the *Watchers/Guardians of the Time Continuum*. That and more. We monitor the timelines and the possible realities."

Steel had a sudden suspicion. "Did you have something to do with the malfunction of our rover?"

"We are the ones who initiated the sequence that rendered your power source useless. We did not mean to cause you any discomfort. We apologize."

"The Gifford and the Steel will be removed from this timeline," said the creature on the chair. "For this, we apologize also."

"What?" Steel stared first at the speaker and then at the man in the shiny uniform.

"We cannot allow you to perish in that explosion. Your continued existence is as important as the success of this project. Your descendants are predestined for greatness." The man smiled. "That is all I can tell you."

"What does he mean when he said we'll be removed from this timeline?" Steel asked.

"Once the terra-forming is completed, you and the Gifford will be in different timelines, you will cease to exist as a unit. We must take you to a timeline far removed from your original ones, where you will be able to live together as one." He smiled again. "You will be happy."

"Do we have a choice?" Melanie asked.

"No." The answer came from the being in the chair. "Our existence depends on this. Ours and yours."

Suddenly the chair and the creature disappeared. The man in the silver suit looked at them. "Come with me, please. I promise, no harm will come to you."

"What about the rover?"

"We will destroy it."

They followed him as he walked toward the bright disk. Before they boarded it, Steel looked one last time at the disappearing sun, as it threw its rays across the churning ocean, painting it blood-red.

The last thing he heard before the door closed behind him was the sound of the waves, crashing against the cliffs.

Melanie stayed silent beside him as they walked down a corridor with cold metallic walls. She reached out suddenly and grabbed his hand. He smiled at her, wondering what was going to happen to them. Would they find a place where they could be happy together, or would they have to wander the timelines searching for happiness? Would they be lost on the Cliffs of Time?

He remembered something he had read somewhere.

Not all who wander are lost.

He squeezed Melanie's hand and strode ahead with confidence.

The End

Orion – The Hunt
by Herbert Grosshans

Chapter One

There were eleven in the hunting party. Nine men and two women. They sat in the inn, waiting impatiently for their guide to arrive.

"May I join you at your table?"

The man, who was sitting alone in the dimly lit corner, shrugged his massive shoulders and looked at the intruder. "Sit down," he said quietly, "but keep your hands on the table, where I can see them."

The other one smiled, displaying a row of sharp, pointy teeth. "I have no harmful intentions," he said, sitting down, "just like to become acquainted."

The big man chuckled, his gray eyes studying the newcomer. They saw the laser gun on the hip and the long knife strapped to the upper left arm, but they also saw the tiny tubes protruding from under the tight sleeves…dart shooters. A popular weapon of the reptilian race.

"I am Zegg," the reptile man said. "Are you in the hunting party?"

"Yes, I am," nodded the big man. "I didn't know the *Brothers of the Egg* enjoyed hunting the elephant-dragon."

The reptilian laughed with a gurgling hissing sound. "Just because the elephant-dragon has scales doesn't mean he is one of our brothers. Yes, we enjoy hunting the beast." He tilted his head. "What makes you take part in the hunt? Is it the adventure, or are you looking for fortune, like some of the others?"

"Both, I guess," smiled the big man. "By the way, my name is Orion, Hektor Orion."

"An Earthman, I presume?"

"Not quite, I was born in the *Sirius System*, but my ancestors came from *Earth*. They colonized the fifth planet, which had no native intelligent life of its own, but proved habitable for humans. So I guess I can safely say that I come from pure Earth-stock. Probably no more or no less than most people on Earth, who have been breeding with hundreds of other humanoid races for many Earth centuries."

"What's the difference?" asked the reptilian. "They all go back to the same egg, just like us, just like all the other inhabitants of the Galactic Wheel. We are all brothers."

Orion smiled. "That's a dangerous statement, friend. It could get you killed."

"I know, you Humans don't believe in the *Universal Brotherhood*."

Orion couldn't help but notice the edge in the reptilian's voice, but he also seemed to detect a tinge of sadness. He wondered briefly if the tall reptile man might be his contact. His alien mind was closed. Without his help, there would be no mental communication, even if Orion tried to break the barrier.

His gaze traveled over to the other members of the party. He knew a lot about them, just by listening to their conversations for the last couple of hours.

Samdor Whyte, short and fat, a businessman. Head of a large concern in the *Alpha Centauri System*. Owner of half a dozen planets…or so he said.

Beside him, a big, savage looking brute. At least two and a half meters tall, huge shoulders, powerful arms. Bred on a high gravity planet for only one purpose…to fight.

Samdor Whyte's personal bodyguard.

The bodyguard's thoughts lay wide open to Orion's careful probing. The merchant's mind displayed nothing. Orion sensed the presence of an artificial shield.

A tall, stunning looking woman sat across from Whyte. Her golden hair cascaded down her pale shoulders and her full breasts were straining against the fabric of her tight-fitting body suit. She called herself Lu-onna. Orion detected a strong mind-shield, the shield of a natural telepath. If she sensed his mind-touch, she didn't show it.

He had seen women like her before. She came from the *Rilian System*, where the women were bred for beauty and trained in the art of sensual delights. They were known all over this part of the galaxy.

The *Rilian System* lay in the Neutral Zone, just like Izzard-Junction, the planet they were on. The Neutral Zone was the lawless region that divided the *Galactic Federation of Humans* and the reptilian Imperium, the *Imperial Nest*. On the other side of the *Galactic Federation* was *The Hive*, the part of the Galaxy inhabited by the *Insectoids*.

The second woman in the party sat at a table with three other men. She could be the agent, but he found no evidence that she was. Her thoughts were also hidden behind an artificial screen.

Orion had never seen people of her kind before. She looked humanoid, tall, with a lithe, well-formed body. Her eyes were large, green, with pupils like a cat, and her ears were pointy, with little tufts of fur at the tips. She wore her black hair short, cropped close to her rounded skull. He saw a long knife inside her right boot. No other weapons were evident, but that didn't mean she didn't have any.

One of the men with her looked like a traveler, a man who drifted from planet to planet, searching for something he would never find. His face looked scarred, his eyes wary. The woman had called him 'Selmond'. His mind seemed to be open, but Orion knew better. He could be a highly trained agent, keeping his real thoughts hidden behind the chatter of routine thoughts.

The same could be said for the others.

Dr. Fortney; a scientist from *Terra*. His mind appeared clear and disciplined, letting no random thoughts clutter up his thinking process. He kept it busy thinking about the local flora and fauna he would find.

The tall, handsome young man with the bright smile was Andrew Trongsan. Playboy, spoiled son of an influential family from one of the many planets of the super giant *Antares*, which lay on the outer fringes of the *Human Federation*.

The necklace he wore hid a thought scrambler. Anyone who tried to read his mind would only receive gibberish.

At another table, two young men sat by themselves, not saying much, just watching the others. Brothers. Twins, by the looks of it. Even though one of them wore a thin mustache, it didn't change his appearance much.

Neither of them carried thought scrambles, their thoughts lay open to Orion's probing. However, that meant nothing. A good telepath could hide himself behind an artificial persona.

Orion could probably have smashed through any of the screens, artificial or natural, but that would have given him away.

He was one of the best agents the government of the *Colonial Worlds of Sol-Terra* had. Not many could match his talents. Nevertheless, there had been one who could have come close, if only there would have been enough time to develop her abilities.

The memory of her brought a lump to his throat. She had been so lovely, so beautiful, so young. *Delina*, his mind-sister.

They had been lovers…more than lovers. No other woman had ever captured his heart the way she had, and he had chosen her to bear his son.

For one year they had been together, been through two assignments. Without her, his body would have been destroyed on Arcturus IV.

The arrival of their guide interrupted his thoughts.

Giles.

Orion could see why the innkeeper called him *Nose*. Even the full, bushy mustache couldn't hide the enormous size of his nose. He wore a sloppy outfit; pants and jacket made from the skins of some animal. A wide brimmed hat covered the top of his head, shading his eyes and a necklace of white, bleached teeth hung around his neck.

He looked like a walking arsenal. Two laser guns and a knife on his hips, a flash-rifle on his back, and a dart pistol strapped to his chest.

He walked in, looked around the tavern, his eyes coming to rest on Orion and Zegg. "You two belong to the party?" Giles's spoke with a deep and rough voice. It matched his big frame.

Orion sensed the thought-scrambler built into the ring the guide wore in his left ear, a device made out of platinum. Very expensive. He wondered why the guide had a need for a thought-scrambler, here on this backwater planet.

His companion, the reptile man answered the guide's question. "Yes, we belong."

Giles gave him a hard look. "A rep," he rasped, disapproving. "Not many of your kind are interested in hunting the elephant-dragon. Why am I honored with your presence?"

Zegg smiled. "On my home world I am considered a great hunter. You are the second human today who questions my presence here."

"I am not questioning your presence, and I don't doubt your abilities as a hunter," Giles said coolly. "I am only surprised, that's all." He turned toward the others. "If you people are ready, then let's get moving."

Orion studied the group thoughtfully. Besides him, there was at least one more natural telepath here. Some of the others had either artificial screens, or scramblers to ensure privacy of their thoughts, or hide something else.

A high percentage of highly qualified people. Very unusual.

Something deep inside him stirred, like a long forgotten ghost, wary and watchful. His thoughts shifted into a higher level.

The primitives are awakening. It won't be long. The Dark Hunters of the Serpent *should not be far away.*

.

Chapter Two

Izzard-Junction was an unexplored planet. Larger then Earth, with a diameter of about 16,000 km, it should have had a higher gravity, but because of its lower density the gravity was still around Earth-norm. Most of its surface was covered by land, with only one large ocean. Much of the land area consisted of deep, impenetrable jungle, broken up by huge lakes and millions of smaller lakes and rivers.

There were natives, lizard-like beings, but they shunned the aliens from outer space. Not much was known about them, except that they were primitive and savage

Nobody had claimed this planet, because it didn't have anything to offer that could not be found on other, more hospitable, planets. A few colonists had settled in the more temperate zones, some left again after years of struggling against the hostile elements, but some had stayed.

The spaceport, also called *Izzard-Junction*, had grown into a city of about 130,000 inhabitants, with a few smaller settlements in the surrounding areas.

There was another large settlement of about 40,000 inhabitants in the Northern Hemisphere, by the ocean. They called it *Makkuo-Tsei*, which means *The Eye of God*. Most of its inhabitants settled there after fleeing from a planet in the *Bellatrix System*, where they had been prosecuted for their religious beliefs.

Their main food supply came from the ocean, which held many varieties of aquatic life forms, some of them so huge and gigantic that they were a menace to the fishing vessels.

Makkuo-Tsei's contact with the rest of *Izzard-Junction* was very limited.

Only because of its location near the center of the Neutral-Zone *Izzard-Junction* had been settled at all.

Since it had no central government, with practically no law, it naturally attracted all kinds of travelers. It became a popular meeting place for criminal elements as well as agents from many stellar worlds, humans and non-humans.

Billions of giant reptiles inhabited the jungles, and many adventure seekers came here for *The Hunt*, which the locals promoted. The most popular quarry was the elephant-dragon, a large reptile with a head like a Terran elephant. The long tasks were of an ivory-like substance and used for carvings, but the most valuable part was the single horn on the forehead of the bulls. Its crystalline structure made it a highly prized commodity on the human worlds for making jewelry. Since diamonds and gold could be manufactured artificially and had been found in vast quantities on hundreds of planets, they had lost their value and attraction.

Elephant-dragons were huge, vicious, and possessed ferocity unequalled by any animal the humans had ever encountered. Hunting them was a treacherous undertaking, and many fortune hunters had lost their lives. They lived in the swamps and were not easy to track, but once aroused they attacked without warning. Their size and fantastic speed made them extremely dangerous, but only added to the attraction searched for by thrill-seeking hunters. After searching the Terran government's computer database, Orion found little information about Izzard-Junction and the Hunt, but what little he did find gave him at least enough to be somewhat informed.

* * * *

They were flying at an altitude of 6,000 meters. Orion estimated their speed at around 900 km/hr, relatively slow, but after a snide remark from Samdor Whyte the guide snapped, "This no speed boat and if you don't like it you can walk the 6,500 km to the swamp regions."

The fat merchant glared at him; TAR-8, his bodyguard, grunted, the bulging muscles on his huge body twitching, his hand touching the hilt of his saber, but after a tense moment Whyte relaxed and touched the bodyguard's arm.

Giles smiled. "Some day I'll get myself a larger, faster boat, but until then this one will have to do."

The aircraft was an old military model, originally intended as a patrol boat. Probably left over from the early days, when *Izzard-Junction* was still under *Space Patrol* law. Someone, probably

Giles, stripped it of its military hardware and remodeled it into a passenger boat. Not as comfortable as a real luxury cruiser, with little room to move around in and much of the space being used for carrying cargo, but the air conditioning worked. Almost the most important thing on this humid planet.

The aircraft shot silently across the lakes and the jungle. A barely audible hum came from the power drive, also an ancient model, used mainly on backward planets that had little contact with the rest of the human populated worlds.

Orion wondered again about Giles, if he could possibly be his contact. He hadn't learned very much about the guide. Apparently, he'd been taking hunters on expeditions into the unexplored regions of this planet for quite some time. According to the innkeeper, Giles was a tough, well-experienced guide, who knew the wild backcountry. He'd grown up on this planet, and he knew how to handle that old rig of his, meaning that he was also a very good pilot; very important when you took trips into unexplored territory.

The innkeeper had called him 'Nose', and not just because of the size his nose. "He seems to smell the presence of his quarry, and he always finds his way out of the deepest jungle. He never gets lost."

He could be the agent, but somehow Orion doubted it. No, it had to be an outsider, one of his companion hunters. His gaze fell on the cat-woman who had chosen the seat beside him. She noticed his eyes and smiled at him.

"I don't think we've been introduced," she said with a guttural low voice, her large green eyes studying him curiously. She swiveled her seat around to face him. "My name is Sheenah." She spoke High-Galact with a peculiar accent.

"Sheenah?" Orion repeated. "A name somewhat popular on Earth."

She smiled. "It is not my real name, but I like it."

"Why not tell me your real name?" Orion asked, somewhat perplexed.

"I don't really have a name," Sheenah explained. "It is not the custom of my people. We recognize each other by different means. It is hard to explain to an outsider." She paused and smiled. "So what can I call you?"

"I am Orion. Hektor Orion," he said.

"Hello, Hektor Orion." Her silvery laughter sounded pleasant to his ears and he found himself strangely attracted to her. She nodded toward the guide. "Quite a character."

Orion grinned. "He sure is, but as long as he finds the dragons, I don't care."

"You've hunted before?"

"Not this beast, but I've hunted on other planets." Not a lie, just half-truth. Oh, yes, he had hunted before, a beast more cunning, more vicious and ruthless than the elephant-dragon, the most dangerous beast in the Galaxy…man.

He was hunting now, trying to find the men who had taken his beautiful Delina from him. He didn't know what they looked like, didn't even know who they were. They might not even be on Izzard-Junction, but their trail had led him to this planet.

The trail of the slave-traders.

Six earth-months had passed since Delina's disappearance from her home-planet Dio-Solis, Vega's fourth planet. Her brother had been brutally murdered by the three men who took her and left her little sister, Ablena, for dead. Ablena survived, but had been unable to tell much, enough for Orion, Delina's mind-brother, to go after the abductors, to hunt them down, to kill, if necessary, and maybe find his Delina again.

Her abduction was only one in a series of thousands of similar incidents all over the Federation, but hers was a special case. She was a government agent for the Colonial Worlds. Orion couldn't understand why she could have let herself be taken, unless…

He didn't want to connect the *Dark Hunters* with her, because then his search would prove to be almost hopeless and deadly.

After feeding all of the available information into the AMN, the Artificial Mind Net, it provided him with a list of possible planets, but all had proved dead ends, so far. The AMN had come up with another connection, told him to join the Hunt on Izzard-Junction and wait for another agent to contact him. A special ring worn on his finger would identify him to his contact.

Looking at the slim young body of the cat-woman, Orion was again painfully reminded of Delina.

"Something troubling you?" Sheenah asked, a concerned look on her alien, pretty face.

Orion gave her a smile, somewhat taken aback. She couldn't have read his mind. He hadn't found any indication that she was a telepath. Of course, her powers of intuition could be very keen. She also might have read it in his face, although he usually controlled his features well. "You remind me of someone I once knew and cared for," he said, realizing she'd know if he lied.

"You must have loved her very much," she said and then she smiled. "Painful memories are best forgotten." She reached out, touching his hand. "I have been watching you and I've tried to figure out what you are. The way you move and talk, the way you look at people. You are not a treasure-seeker, nor are you looking for adventure." Her voice dropped to almost a whisper. "It's your eyes that give you away, Hektor. You are a hunter, but not of animals. You hunt men!"

Orion's gray eyes narrowed, his senses alert. How did she know?

Her hand squeezed his. He could feel her tremble. Then she whispered, "Have you killed many men? Any women?"

Now he understood. She didn't know anything about him. She just possessed a highly developed sense of observation and guessed the rest. He also knew why she took part in the hunt. Bloodlust.

"Yes, I have killed," he said slowly, "and I didn't enjoy it. You're wrong about one thing...I am here only to hunt the elephant-dragon, nothing else." He watched her closely as she stretched her lithe body lazily, her cat's eyes bright with apparent excitement. It could also be a cover.

She didn't answer, just smiled and wiggled her pointy ears, looking extremely attractive and seductive.

Orion leaned back in his seat, closing his eyes. He seemed relaxed and untroubled, but his built-in sentries were working overtime.

Chapter Three

Orion could feel the plane dropping lower. A look out of the window confirmed it. The ground rushed up toward them, the aircraft leveled, slowed and hovered over a bare, rocky area. To one side, a huge swamp stretched for kilometers, on the other side rose the giant trees of the jungle. Beyond the jungle in the hazy distance, Orion caught occasional glimpses of a snow-covered mountain ridge.

The craft touched ground and the humming of the drive quit abruptly, leaving an almost uncomfortable silence.

Giles stretched and turned toward his passengers, who had begun to get out of their seats. "Just hold it a moment. Nobody steps outside until I say so," he rasped. "I saw a small herd of the dragons deep in the swamp. They're heading this way, but we'll have to wait, they won't be here for at least a couple of hours. We have enough time to get ready for them."

"How do you know they'll come here?" Selmond, the traveler, challenged him.

Giles stared at him for a moment. "So you do talk," he snorted. "For a while I thought you had no voice, since so far everybody had something to complain about." He paused for a moment. "This place we've landed on is a giant rock at the edge of the swamp, the only dry place for hundreds of square kilometers. "He pointed out of the window. "If you'll take the trouble to look outside, you'll find the ground covered with large and small boulders. The dragons like to lie between those rocks and bask in the sun. All we have to do is wait for them and take our pick."

"Sounds simple," one of the twin-brothers commented, "but I bet it isn't."

Giles chuckled deep in his throat. "You're right, smart boy, quite right. These beasts are not stupid, and they don't like to be disturbed. We'll have to camouflage this craft and then we'll hide in the jungle. We let them come ashore and settle down, let them rest and calm down. While they do that we wait."

"Wait for what?" Samdor Whyte, the merchant, asked loudly. "What kind of hunting is that? I've hunted wild beasts on many planets and that's not the way I hunt. Once I have my quarry in my sights I pull the trigger."

"You'll do that and you're a dead man. A stupid dead man!"

TAR-8 growled and moved toward the guide, but the merchant held him back. "Wait," he said hoarsely, "maybe later I'll let you take this insolent bastard apart, but for now we'll still need him." Turning toward Giles, he said, "So we wait, and then what?"

"About an hour before sundown they'll move back into the swamp. The young ones and the females go first, then the bulls. The largest bull is last, and that's when we move in for the kill. You see, once the others are in the swamp, they won't turn back, no matter what happens to the lead bull. He'll have to look out for himself." The guide spoke calmly and patiently, but Orion saw him watching the big giant.

"Sounds logical but not dangerous," Sheenah said.

"Just follow my instructions and we'll have no problems." Giles got up and pulled a bundle from one of the compartments above the seats. "Get into your gear and don't forget to rub all your exposed parts with insect repellant, unless you want to be eaten alive."

They were busy for a while getting dressed, and then they stepped outside. The sun stood already quite high, and after being in the cool fresh air of the aircraft, the hot humid air hit them like a blast from a furnace.

All of them wore tight-fitting outfits with built-in cooling units. Orion adjusted the controls and felt more comfortable immediately.

Zegg, the reptilian, seemed to be the only one, besides the guide, who didn't appear bothered by the heat and humidity. He stood smiling in the hot sun, with his arms outstretched. The fine scales on his skin shimmered like polished silver in the bright light. "Ah," he sighed. "Just like home."

"Let's go," grumbled Giles, "we have much to do before we are safe. Don't waste time sunning yourself."

They covered the entire aircraft with a finely meshed metallic cover. When they were finished, it looked like a giant boulder. After that they moved into the jungle and spread out, hiding close to the edge, just far enough into the dense foliage to be protected from the rays of the sun.

"Don't go too deep into the jungle," Giles warned them. "There are all kinds of dangers lurking in there. So stay close and within sight of each other."

Orion made himself comfortable beside a large rock, when somebody else squatted down beside him. He looked up and recognized Sheenah.

"Do you mind?" she asked.

He shook his head. "No, I don't mind the company." He smiled. "Your company."

Her eyes were large and bright. "This is so exciting," she whispered and then she leaned against him. "Do you think we'll be lucky?"

He shrugged. "I don't know. We'll just have to wait and see."

"Is there a possibility somebody might get hurt?" she asked breathlessly, but Orion didn't get a chance to reply.

"Quiet over there!" Giles called out harshly. "You can talk all you want later, but for now shut up!"

Orion smiled when the cat-woman growled angrily, somehow grateful for the guide's interruption.

They could hear the coming of the great beasts long before they saw them. The trumpeting of the bulls carried a long distance. Orion strained his eyes to catch a glimpse of the herd as it sloshed through the swamp toward the rock and when he finally did see them the animals seemed small, but he know that was an illusion. As they came closer, the hissing and trumpeting became almost ear shattering, and when they climbed onto land, the ground shook, as if rocked by an earthquake.

Orion marveled at the size of the beasts. The smallest one was about three meters long and stood one meter at the shoulders. The lead bull looked enormous, at least 25 meters long from head to tail, plus another five meters for the trunk. The prized horn on its head was no less than seven meters off the ground.

Orion counted ten young ones of all sizes, eight females and three bulls. The other two bulls were not much smaller than the lead bull.

After the initial noisy arrival, they soon quieted down and it didn't take long before they were sleeping in the sun, unmoving and uncaring, secure in the knowledge that nothing would disturb their sleep. They were the undisputed kings of this world.

Chapter Four

The sun hung low above the horizon, throwing long shadows, when the giant reptiles began to stir. The young ones started chasing each other among the rocks, squealing and hissing loudly, while the females tried to herd them back toward the swamp.

Orion crouched behind his rock, trying to get the circulation back into his cramped legs. He poked the cat-woman, who had fallen asleep, gently in the ribs. She came awake instantly, bearing her teeth in an instinctive defensive gesture, but then she smiled. "Is it time?"

"Yes," Orion whispered. "They are going back into the swamp."

Most of the great beasts were already splashing in the water, moving away from the rock. One of the bulls had followed them also, and the lead bull stood watching as the second one moved toward the swamp. Not until all of them were safely away from the rocks would the lead bull follow.

Orion had his laser rifle ready, the soft spot behind the dragon's armored head plate in his sight. Any moment now, Giles would give the signal.

Orion heard a sudden loud crack and then the angry trumpeting sound of the elephant-dragon. The huge beast reared up, clawing the air with its powerful front legs.

"Who the hell was that?" Giles roared.

Two figures appeared out of the jungle and crouching they ran toward the angrily hissing behemoth.

Orion recognized the short fat body of the merchant and his bodyguard TAR-8. Both of them stopped at the same time and fired their heavy lasers again.

"Those fools will get themselves killed," yelled Selmond, jumped up from his hiding place and ran after them. Another figure followed him closely, large breasts jiggling inside the tight-fitting outfit...Lu-onna.

They had managed to hit the dragon, but even the laser rifles didn't do much damage if they burned only armored plate or muscles. Right now, they faced an angry beast, looking for the cause of its discomfort.

The gaze of its large shimmering eyes fastened on Lu-onna who had started running to the next boulder. Before the angry bull made a move in her direction, Selmond stood up and fired a shot at its raised trunk, then he turned and ran in the direction of the hidden aircraft.

Orion heard Giles cursing loudly as he watched Selmond disappear under the craft's covering. The elephant-dragon, who had followed the adventurer, stood hissing and roaring in front of the disguised aircraft. With a loud trumpeting roar, it raised its trunk and smashed it down.

The noise of breaking glass and collapsing metal brought on another string of curses from the guide.

Now the dragon reared up on its hind legs, and then it came down hard right on top of the aircraft, trumpeting angrily. The protective covering slipped off and exposed the smashed middle section of the craft. Discovering the gleaming metal, the mad beast backed off, lowered its huge armored head and started rolling the aircraft toward the swamp.

The craft finally fell into the water, the whole front of it was a mass of smashed instruments and broken metal.

With a final note of triumph, the bull-dragon trumpeted loudly and slid into the swamp, leaving behind a disappointed group of hunters and a very mad guide.

"I told you to wait for my signal, you stupid, fat spawn of a castrated lizard!" he yelled at Samdor Whyte, who was still firing after the disappearing animal.

Giles grabbed the merchant's shoulders and spun him around. "You damn fool, look what you did by not following my orders!"

Whyte shook off the guide's hand, his face a cold white mask. "I don't follow anybody's orders," he whispered hoarsely and snapped his fingers. "He's all yours, TAR-8."

The giant pulled out a long knife and advanced toward the guide, who backed off slowly.

"You'd better call him back," Giles said, watching his adversary with narrowed eyes. "If anything happens to me, you are all dead. Only I can get you away from here."

"He is right, you know," Lu-onna said, touching the merchant's arm. "Without him we are lost."

"You stay out of it!" Whyte said, shooting her an angry look. "From now on I am in charge. I, who control the lives of millions of people, will not be intimidated by a slimy little backwater snake. I've been in worse situations than this." Turning to his bodyguard, he said, "Kill him!"

TAR-8's right arm shot back, but before he could throw his knife, Giles moved in. Orion saw the flash of steel and heard the gurgling sound. Then he watched the guide step back to leave the giant spurting blood from his slit throat. As if to complete the job, Giles now held a dart-pistol in his hand and shooting from the hip, he put a dart into the bodyguard's wide chest. Without a sound, the giant fell to the ground, kicked for a few moments, and then he lay still.

Dr. Fortney looked horrified at the blood-covered body. Then he turned away, retching. "Barbarians," he murmured. "They will never change."

Orion felt long fingers digging painfully into his arm and turned toward the cat-woman who also stared at the dead giant. Her large feline eyes seemed to glow and her breathing had quickened. "So much excitement over nothing," she whispered.

Giles looked around, his dart-pistol still in his hands. "Any more complaints?" he asked.

Whyte stood silent, his face ashen. Orion could sense the hate even through the artificial mind-shield.

The two twins seemed subdued and didn't comment.

The guide looked at the mangled wreck of the aircraft and at the tail end sticking out of the murky water. "I'm sure the communication equipment is destroyed, which means we have no way of calling for assistance. The closest settlement is approximately fifty kilometers north of here. They don't have much communication with the outside world, but we can call for help from there."

"How will we get there?" Lu-onna asked.

Giles threw an annoying glance at the blonde buxom woman,

as if blaming her for the predicament they were in. "The jungle seems impenetrable, but there are many trails, which we can follow. We will leave first thing in the morning. Luckily, the luggage compartment looks undamaged. There is camping gear in the plane. We will salvage what we can now, before the aircraft vanishes in the swamp." He looked at the disappearing sun. "Let's hurry it up. We don't have much time."

He walked toward the swamp. The others followed reluctantly. A huge hole gaped in the top of the plane. Giles turned to Orion. "You, big man, help me getting the stuff out!"

They found Selmond's battered body inside the aircraft, his eyes open, already glazing over. He looked almost peaceful.

"Maybe he finally found what he was searching for," Orion said quietly. Giles gave him a strange look, but said nothing.

Chapter Five

The group left at daybreak. They followed a fairly wide trail winding through the thick vegetation. The trees reached almost a thousand meters into the sky and not much light filtered through the heavy foliage, but all of them carried headlamps with a nearly inexhaustible power supply.

Twice they had to move out of the way when a group of large animals came galloping down the trail. The first time it was half a dozen lizard-like creatures, and the second time a long line of giant birds ran past them, clucking excitedly.

Giles shot the last one.

"They make good eating," he said, grinning with great satisfaction, as he butchered his kill. "Better than those synthetic food tablets you're carrying."

"Speaking of eating," said Andrew Trongsan. "How about stopping for a rest? I think we all could use it."

Giles nodded. "Alright, let's stop for awhile. It's almost noon, anyway." He finished cutting off a chunk of meat from the big bird's breast and handed it to Zegg. "Here, start preparing this and one of you start a fire."

The reptilian shook his head, smiling faintly. "Better let someone else handle it. I am a vegetarian."

Orion stepped forward and took the meat from the guide. "I'll do it," and, turning toward Zegg, he said, "You are full of surprises. Those teeth could have fooled me."

Zegg laughed and sat down. Leaning his back against the root of one of the giant trees, he folded his legs under him. "I do eat meat, but only on certain occasions."

"I've heard of members of your species eating Humans," Giles said.

"And I have heard of humans eating humans," countered the reptilian, chewing on a food-stick.

Trongsan began clearing away leafs and vegetation and lit a fire, while Orion cut the meat into small chunks, which he speared onto long reeds cut from the center of a fern-like plant.

The others made themselves comfortable around the fire and held their chunks of meat into the flames. When Orion bit off a piece from his share, he found the meat tasty, but somewhat gamy.

After everyone finished eating, Giles decided they had rested enough and ordered them to move on.

The rest of the day went by without any memorable incidents. Everyone seemed in good spirits, except for Whyte, who complained about everything, cursing Giles for killing his bodyguard, who could have carried his backpack. Lu-onna tried to calm him down, but he told her to shut up.

The air was hot and humid. Even with their air-conditioned suits, they felt extremely uncomfortable.

Orion wiped his sweat-covered face and swatted at the insects that tried to find a spot on his skin he might have missed covering with repellant. He glanced at Sheenah, who walked stoically beside him. "How are you holding out?"

She gave him a cynical smile. "How do you think?" she asked, throwing an angry look at the fat merchant walking ahead of them. "If it weren't for that fat *selkos,* we wouldn't be in this situation. I joined this hunt to experience some adventure, but this is a little bit too much excitement even for me. I had planned to spend the night inside the safety and comfort of the aircraft." She touched his arm and chuckled. "And maybe in the strong arms of a fellow hunter."

He grinned at her. "That could still be arranged."

According to Orion's timepiece and his legs, they had walked over eight hours. When he looked up, he didn't see any light shining through the branches and giant leafs above them.

Giles called for a halt and told them to begin clearing an area beside the trail where they could set up their tents. Orion crawled into his, tired and glad to finally rest for a while.

The tent material had been treated with a chemical repellant, which would keep away insects and even smaller animals. Giles set up an electronic detection device that would activate an alarm if some large animal decided to come too close to their sleeping quarters, eliminating the need for a guard.

Even though the night was alive with many strange and eerie sounds, Orion slept quite well.

* * * *

The next day did not bring much change. By evening, the path suddenly ended and they entered a large clearing, bare of vegetation. When Orion looked up, he could see a patch of sky through the overhanging branches. The reason for the lack of vegetation became clear when he looked at the ground. Solid rock.

The sound of splashing water indicated a spring and they soon found the small stream flowing in the middle of the clearing, fed by water gushing out of the ground.

"We'll camp here for the night," Giles said and laid his pack against the trunk of a small tree. "The water is clear and fresh and the sky is a welcome sight."

Nobody argued with him. Everyone was tired, thirsty and hungry. They erected their tents and put their packs inside. Zegg began searching for dry branches and made a fire, but he shook his head when Giles offered him a piece of the leftover bird meat.

Orion washed his face and hands in the cold water of the stream, and then he joined the others sitting around the campfire and listened to Giles talking about past hunts. When darkness fell, he crawled into his tent for another, hopefully, peaceful night.

He lay awake for a while, listening to the soft whispering and giggling coming from Whyte's tent, which stood close to his own. Once in awhile he heard the soft cries of a woman…Lu-onna's. Orion smiled, feeling somewhat envious. That woman certainly knew how to keep a man stimulated. He fell asleep, in his mind the image of the fat merchant moving between Lu-onna's widespread fleshy thighs.

He awoke, his defense system ready to strike, when he sensed the presence of someone sliding into his tent. He lay quietly and carefully sent a weak searching mental tentacle toward the intruder's mind. When he touched the artificial shield he smiled and relaxed, watching the slim shadow gliding up beside him.

"Don't pretend you're sleeping. I know you are awake," she whispered into his ear. "I can see quite well in the dark." Her cat's eyes glowed softly above him.

Orion chuckled and reached for her. She was already easing out of her clothes and moments later boldly pulled down his pants. "You certainly are not shy," he said and stroked the cat-woman's round buttocks as she slid on top of him. Her skin was covered with fine, incredibly silky fuzz. It sent waves of delicate pleasure through him from every spot where their naked bodies touched. Her warm breasts pressed into his chest, soft and warm.

She made a guttural sound deep in her throat, touched his erect penis, curled her fingers around it and eased herself onto it. "Ahh..." she moaned softly. "You are big all over. It feels good"

He could feel the soft bushy mass of hair growing around her groin area as she moved against him and dug his fingers into her solid buttocks.

From the tent beside him, he could hear the laboring breathing of Samdor Whyte and Lu-onna's ecstatic moans. They were either still at it or again. Orion couldn't be sure. He didn't know how long he had slept. They would probably go on for most of the night. Orion knew about Lu-onna. Women of her race were trained well in the arts of sexual delights. They could keep a man in ecstasy for a long time, using their bodies and all kinds of stimulants on their lips, their nipples and inside their vaginas.

His attention shifted back to Sheenah, the woman in his arms. She had stepped up her speed, moving like a piston on top of him, her slippery sheath holding his throbbing penis in a tight grip.

"Ahh..." She suppressed a cry, just mewed softly. Suddenly she stopped moving, only her love channel seemed alive, milking...pulling...sucking. She raked his back with sharp nails, probably drawing blood, and buried her teeth in his shoulder.

When he shot his discharge into her, she cried out and shook violently above him. He broke through her artificial mind shield and touched her mind at the peak of her orgasm, bringing her climax to highs she probably never experienced before.

She bucked uncontrollably and whimpered loudly in the throes of her orgasm, and then she collapsed and lay exhausted in his arms.

After awhile she stirred and kissed him tenderly, her pointy teeth teasing his tongue.

Orion smiled, feeling quite peaceful and satisfied. She fell asleep in his arms, radiating a content feeling.

He came awake again when he felt her warm, searching hand between his legs. Her lips traveled down his nude body, across his stomach, down to his groin and then very tenderly her lips engulfed him, sucking gently, her tongue teasing the tip of his penis.

More than ready by now, he eased out of her mouth and pulled her up. Then he turned her around. She knelt beside him, her buttocks up and her legs slightly spread. He moved behind her and, carefully, he entered her from behind, sliding easily into her moist, warm sex-organ. She started bucking almost immediately, her need for him seemingly great and insatiable, but when his penis began throbbing, telegraphing his eruption, she moaned deeply and pushed backward, clamping her sheath tightly around his spurting member. Then she sank to the ground, her body limp.

Orion collapsed on top of her, breathing harshly. She turned her head and smiled, her eyes large. "You have many talents," she murmured. "I haven't felt this good for a long time."

He stroked her nude body, soft under his touch, and laughed. "You're not without talent yourself. If we keep this up, you'll wear me out."

She twisted under him and gathered him in her arms, kissing him on the mouth. "I know you and I are from two different species, but if you don't mind, for the duration of this trip I'd like to do this a few more times."

He said nothing, just nodded, knowing she could see him in the dark, and kissed one of her long nipples, sucking it lightly. He noticed for the first time three small bumps with short nipples under each of her breasts and planted a kiss on each one of them.

They lay silent after that, content in each other's arms. Neither of them slept much anymore.

"It seems to get light outside," Orion said. "I guess it's time to get up. We'd better get dressed."

"I don't think anybody is up yet," Sheenah murmured lazily. "I'd like to clean myself before I get dressed. I'm going down to the stream. Want to come?"

She slid out of the tent. He followed close behind, slapping her on her bare buttock. She laughed gaily and ran toward the pond further down.

Orion watched the smooth muscles rippling on her lithe body.

What a magnificent creature. She would make a good companion.

Then he shook his head. *She is not for me. Too different.*

Chapter Six

By the time he arrived at the pond, she was already splashing in the clear water. He stuck his foot into the water and pulled it back, shuddering.

"How can you dive into this?" He rubbed his hands over his naked skin, shivering in the cold morning air.

The cat-woman came out of the pond, dripping, and rubbed her round breasts against him. Even though she had cooled off in the water, her skin felt hot.

"You are covered with goose bumps," she said, laughing.

"Your body temperature must be higher than mine," he said, enjoying her body heat and holding her tightly. "You make me hot all over."

She laughed coyly and dropped a hand between his legs. "What's this? Didn't I satisfy you last night?" She giggled and, with a sudden twist, she freed herself and gave him a push.

Caught off balance, he fell into the icy water. He came up, a little angry at first, but when she slid beside him and came into his arms, his anger subsided quickly. "I hope that cooled you off." She smiled. "We wouldn't want to tell the whole camp what goes on around here."

"That's not necessary," said a giggling voice from shore. "We know already."

They both looked up at the newcomer.

Lu-onna.

Orion stared at her nude golden body, as she slowly walked into the water. Her breasts were even larger and more magnificent than he had imagined. She saw his eyes and she made a show of turning sideways to give him a better view.

"We heard you two last night." She giggled. "Must have been quite a night." She stopped, her breasts floating just above the water line.

Sheenah looked at her coldly, her eyes narrow slits. "Listen to who's talking. You should have heard yourself, you and that fat *selcos* you've been fucking all night. At least I had a real man."

She gave Orion a sidelong glance. "And he had a real woman."

Orion saw the sudden glint in Lu-onna's eyes. "What is that supposed to mean?" she asked with a chilled voice.

"You know what I mean," the cat-woman shot back. "Everything on me is real. I need no help to make a man feel good. But look at yourself. Look at those huge, soft mammary of yours. Disgusting. Unreal. I know about your kind, the aphrodisiacs you use, the tricks you play. You're nothing but a whore!" She spat into the water. "I could take you apart blindfolded and with my hand tied behind my back."

Lu-onna stared at her coldly for a moment. Orion expected her to flare up, maybe drop her mind shield, but she kept it up, never for a moment lost control. Suddenly, she laughed and ducked under the water, wetting her long golden hair. Then she turned and waded to shore, her nude perfect body glistening golden in the morning light filtering through the trees. He noted the sway of her hips and the rounded shape of her buttocks.

Orion heaved a silent sigh. He knew what she could do with that body of hers.

"I guess we'd better get back to camp before we get any more visitors," he said.

Sheenah nodded, pouting. "She spoiled it, that bitch," she said. "I had hoped we could have some more fun in the water, but now I'm not in the mood anymore."

He slapped her on the rump and laughed. "I thought you wanted me to cool off." He grabbed her breasts from behind and kissed her lightly between the shoulder blades. "There is still tonight."

She wriggled against him, rolling his penis between her buttocks. "You're right," she said and smiled, her anger forgotten.

When they got back to the campsite, the others were already up. Giles crouched on the ground, trying to get a fire going. "You could have brought some water for a pot of caf," he grumbled.

Sheenah stood in front of him, arms spread. "Does it look like I could have carried it somewhere on my body? Maybe I should have hid it in here." She pointed to the thick bush of black hair between her legs.

The guide looked her up and down, his face expressionless. "Get dressed!" he rasped.

"Why?" The cat-woman laughed, moving her hips enticingly. "Don't you find me attractive without clothing or is it that you don't like women?" She smiled sweetly, exposing two sharp, tiny fangs. "I've heard stories about men like you, who spend most of their time in the wilderness. Rumors have it that some men, for lack of female partners, sometimes mate with animals or even plants. There is the story about this hermit who lived for many years in the company of a half-sentient plant-woman. Apparently, she satisfied his sexual needs better than any humanoid female ever could have done."

Giles stared at her for a long moment, and then he stood up, grabbed a small container and walked to the stream. Sheenah threw back her head and laughed. "If you feel the urge coming, Big Nose," she called after him, "let me know. You are pretty fast with your knife and your pistols. I wonder if you shoot all of your weapons that fast."

Orion finished dressing and handed Sheenah her clothing. "You shouldn't do that to him," he chided her gently. "He probably hasn't seen a naked woman for some time, at least not one as attractive as you. He is only a man, whatever else he may be. I've noticed him looking at you."

"Getting jealous?" she asked, smiling.

Orion glanced at Andrew Trongsan who seemed busy packing up his gear and apparently not interested in anything else, but Orion had caught him staring at Sheenah when he thought himself unobserved. Even the two brothers had been showing more than a fleeting interest when she came prancing back to the camp stark naked.

"You'd better watch yourself," he warned her. "Men can get pretty ugly when a woman teases them."

"I can take care of myself," she purred. "Besides, there is always you."

He smiled ruefully. "I could get killed. Accidents happen."

She chuckled deep in her throat and slowly dressed herself, oblivious to the glances the men threw in her direction.

"Come and get your caf," Giles called after throwing some leaves into the boiling water.

Orion walked over to the fire and poured himself a cup. The guide watched him silently, sipping on his own cup. "Since she seems to have taken a fancy to you, Orion," he said after awhile in a quiet voice, "you keep her on the leash. That woman needs some taming." He spat, spilled the rest of his caf into the fire and turned toward his gear.

"Let's get a move on now. We have a long way to go."

Orion finished packing his stuff and slung the pack over his shoulders. He looked up at the sky, where dark clouds were beginning to gather.

Giles noticed his look and came over, shouldering his own pack. "We might get some bad weather today," he said to Orion. "These storms can get quite nasty." He called to the others. "Gather around for a minute."

Chapter Seven

"I did some rock-climbing when I was young but I'm not sure if I can climb a tree." Dr. Fortney shook his head and craned his neck to look up into the thicket above them.

"I'm not exactly fond of heights," one of the twins said, "but I think we can manage. The bark on these trees is rough. There are many footholds and it shouldn't be too difficult."

"I've done a lot of climbing. Rocks and trees," Sheenah said. "There's nothing to it. You just have to overcome your fear of heights. Once we're in the trees, those branches are so wide it'll be like walking on the ground."

"Well, I guess you just volunteered to take the lead," Giles said.

"I guess I did." Sheenah removed her shoes, stowed them in her backpack and approached the huge tree trunk. Reaching up to grab hold of a piece of bark, she began climbing. Orion noted her long toes, like fingers almost, and the way she used them to push herself up.

"Not everyone has toes like that," the twin with the mustache commented. "She's a natural tree dweller."

"Her ancestors probably were," his brother added to his comment.

Orion had to agree. She did look like one born in the trees. She scaled the side of the tree trunk with apparent ease and soon she disappeared among the thick vines and large leaves that covered the craggy surface of the giant tree.

"Give me a moment and I'll throw down a rope," she called from within the deep foliage. Her voice sounded muffled.

The end of a rope appeared and began snaking its way down the trunk. Giles grabbed it and gave a gentle pull. "I hope you secured it tightly. We don't want anyone falling because you were negligent," he yelled up at her.

"If you don't trust me then stay down there," Sheenah yelled back.

Giles turned to the group. "Alright, who wants to go first?"

"I'll go," Orion said and tied the rope to the broad belt he had taken from his pack. Staring into the foliage above him, he called to Sheenah, "I'm coming up. Start pulling me up, but do it slowly." Then he began climbing. Even with his boots on he had no trouble finding footholds in the deep crevices between the rough bark, but without the safety of the rope he may not have felt as confident climbing the steep surface as he did.

Sheenah kept the rope tight, which helped him tremendously. A few times, he almost slipped on slippery patches of lichen, but he didn't hurry, always made sure he had a good grip with both hands, before he moved his feet.

The backpack pulled heavily, threatened to drag him backwards.

Once he looked down at the eagerly watching group below him and wished he hadn't. They appeared so small and distant. When he finally reached the safety of the shelf Sheenah crouched on, he felt exhausted. She held onto the rope until he was safely sitting beside her. Then she gave him a happy smile and touched his nose with one finger. "Glad to see you, big man," she said. "Maybe we should just forget about the others, huh?"

He grinned at her. "Maybe. But we'd be stuck up here forever."

"You're right." She laughed. "Let's bring 'em up."

Orion checked the rope, satisfied that it was secure, and then he lowered it down. "Send up your packs first," he called through the thicket.

It took some time until someone finally yanked on the rope. Sheenah helped him pulling the rope and soon they had four of the packs beside them. Twice more they lowered the rope until they had all the packs.

"We'll have to make some room first," Orion called down. "Give us a moment."

About twenty meters above them a bulge in the tree surface signaled another natural shelf, large enough to stow the packs. Orion took a rope out of his pack and handed it to Sheenah, who began climbing without saying another word.

"How does it look?" Orion asked her after she disappeared

over the top of the bulge.

"Good," she called down, leaning out so he could see her head. "There is a chunk of tree missing. Looks like some animal chewed on it. The opening is large enough to bring everyone up."

"Alright. Now throw me the rope."

Once all the packs were stowed away on the upper shelf, Sheenah clambered back down and joined him. Making sure again the rope was still secure Orion threw the end down to the waiting group.

Lu-onna was the first one they pulled up. To Orion's amazement, she didn't even seem out of breath when she crawled onto the shelf. "Not as bad as I thought." She smiled at Orion.

Sheenah gave her a poisonous look. "I'm surprised you didn't rub off your big tits on the bark," she hissed.

"I'm happy to see you, too," Lu-onna said. She looked up. "I see you've left a rope hanging from our next resting place. Mind if I just go ahead?"

"Be my guest," Sheenah said sourly. "I won't catch you if you fall."

"Don't worry. I won't."

She took a hold of the rope and climbed up to the next shelf. Orion was happy to have her out of the way. With the animosity between the two women, an accident was bound to happen.

Trongsan was next and then Dr. Fortney. The older man seemed in good spirits. "I guess I'm in better shape than I thought," he said, grinning like a schoolboy. He lay down on the narrow shelf, breathing heavily. "But I think I'll need a bit of rest before I can go on."

"I'm sending up Whyte," Giles called from below. "Better brace yourself and hang on to the rope."

"Give me a hand," Orion said to Trongsan, who nodded and stood beside Orion as they hauled up the fat merchant.

"I don't think he's climbing at all," Trongsan puffed. "Like pulling up a mountain of lard."

Sheenah laughed behind them. "What did you think you were bringing up?"

They couldn't see Whyte, but they could sure hear him

cursing.

"Maybe you should drop him," Sheenah said. "It'll make a good splash."

The merchant looked green by the time they pulled him onto the shelf. Cursing he squatted down beside Dr. Fortney. "I didn't pay to be humiliated like this." He could barely catch his breath. "Heads will roll when I get back to my world."

"If you get back," Dr. Fortney said softly.

Orion threw the rope down again. The next two who arrived were the two brothers. As usual they didn't speak much, just asked if they should climb higher.

"Go ahead," Orion told them. "Perhaps you can help Dr. Fortney and Whyte to get to the next shelf. Lu-onna is already up there."

Giles didn't give them any problems. The reptile man, Zegg, followed closely behind the guide. He hadn't bothered with the rope. His sharp teeth shone white in the semidarkness when he climbed onto the shelf.

"I didn't want to brag about my abilities," he said. "Action is stronger than mere words."

Once everyone reached the second shelf, they decided to take a rest for a while.

"How high do we have to climb?" asked Dr. Fortney.

"Until we reach the thick branches that interconnect the trees with each other," Giles said.

"And how high will that be?"

"How about another 250 meters?" The guide grinned as if enjoying what he just told everyone.

"Two hundred and fifty meters?" exclaimed Whyte. "I'll be dead before then."

"Maybe just as well," Giles rumbled. "At least then I won't have to listen to your whining." He glared at the merchant. "Remember whose fault it is that we are up here in the first place?"

"Can't we stop this bickering? It is not good for the morale. Things just happened, there's nothing we can do about it now. Let us look forward and maybe we'll survive this."

Orion looked at the young man who spoke up so bravely. "You know," he said, "you're absolutely right. By the way, I don't think we've been introduced. What's your name?"

"It's Harriss, Trevor Harriss, and my brother's name is Ross."

"I'm Hektor. You two are twins, correct?"

Trevor grinned. "Identical. That's why he's got the mustache."

"What made you join the hunt?"

"The same reason everyone else did, I guess." Trevor shrugged.

"And what would that be? Adventure?"

"That and the promise of becoming rich. Right, brother." Trevor looked at his brother who had stayed silent.

Ross nodded slowly. "Right. What else?"

"Enough chit-chat," Giles rose to his feet. "I don't want to get caught sitting here in the open when the storm hits."

Sheenah and Zegg climbed side by side to the next stop, the first branch, wide and thick, but not reaching far. They let down two ropes and helped the others as they crawled slowly up the sheer wall. When one of the twin-brothers almost tumbled backwards after grabbing a vine that broke under his weight, Giles warned him, not to trust the illusive safety of the vegetation. Even though the vines looked strong and solid, they weren't, and neither were the large leaves.

By the time everyone was safely resting on the rough, but relatively flat surface of the branch, the first indication that the storm had begun came when a few large drops of water fell through the upper branches.

Giles studied the vegetation above them. "We'll have to climb up to the next branch. We won't be safe on this one."

That branch didn't point in the right direction and neither did the next two.

"I don't know if I can climb any higher today," Whyte groaned. "I can't feel my limbs."

"Maybe you should have saved your energy last night," Sheenah sneered. "You can't fuck all night and expect to climb trees the next day."

"Oh, shut up, you furry parody of a woman!" Whyte growled.

"Enough!" Giles roared. "This is not helping. Everybody up. Now!"

"I don't take orders from you!" The fat man glared at the guide.

"Then you stay behind. Simple as that."

Again, the cat-woman and the reptilian were the first to climb. The water running along the trunk of the tree made it slippery and treacherous. Orion found it difficult to find a good foothold in the slimy cracks, his boots kept on slipping, and he felt thankful for the rope that kept him from falling a few times.

The branch he stood on looked wider and safer than the ones below them, but the rainwater from above and the lichen and moss promised a perilous journey. They clicked pieces of rope into their belts to keep one connected to another and started walking on the broad surface of the branch.

The water from the upper branches came down heavier now and soon the bark under Orion's feet became so slippery he knew it was just a matter of time before someone slipped and went over.

He could hear the roaring of the storm through the heavy vegetation above them and felt the vibration of the swaying upper branches. It had also become darker and without their headlamps, they would have not been able to see much.

"We'll have to tie ourselves down," Giles yelled suddenly. He unclipped his rope from Orion's belt and proceeded to wrap it around a branch that grew out of the large one they stood on.

Orion turned toward the cat-woman who was on the other end of his rope, when someone cried out. His reflexes took over his body and, without thinking, he hooked his left hand into the belt of Dr. Fortney who stood close beside him and threw his right arm around a sturdy branch nearby. Fortney's rope was tied to Sheenah's on one end and his other end clicked into Whyte's belt.

Moments later Orion felt the terrible wrenching as the rope that held the merchant tightened. Then he saw the fat man dangling below them, cursing loudly and screaming for help.

Lu-onna, who had been on the other end of Whyte's rope, was tangled up in some lose vines, hanging on, but she was losing her precarious hold. Luckily, Zegg had also been on the alert. He just finished wrapping the slack of his rope around a heavy branch. Trongsan clung to a clump of vines for dear life.

In the meantime, the rain had become extremely heavy and the increasing darkness added to the danger.

"Get me the hell up there, you morons," Whyte bellowed from below.

"If you don't shut up we'll just cut the ropes," roared Giles. "Maybe you can grow wings and fly up."

Making sure his rope was still securely tied to the branch, he slowly inched toward Orion and helped him hold the rope that held the merchant. Meanwhile, the cat-woman had released her rope from Dr. Fortney's belt and from Orion's, then she tied her own rope to Giles' branch and crawled over to where Lu-onna kept her shaky hold onto the lose vines.

"Untie Whyte's rope end from your belt, Lu-onna," Orion called to her. "We've got him secure now. If you go down we might lose you both."

"I can't do it," Lu-onna answered weakly. "I need both my hands just to hold our weight. Samdor is not a light man."

"We have him," Giles called. "He won't fall if you cut him loose."

"I don't know what you see in him, anyway," Sheenah said. She had managed to climb down to Lu-onna's position. Reaching out, she unclipped the merchant's rope, slightly pulling up, the she called, "Watch out, fat man," and let go of the rope.

Whyte let out a hoarse yell when he suddenly dropped further down, but Orion and Giles held him safely. When they tried to pull him up, they found it extremely difficult. Whyte was nothing but dead weight swinging in free air.

"We need some help here," Giles called out.

"Maybe we can help," the twins spoke at the same time. "What can we do?" one of them asked.

"Throw him one end of your rope so he can grab it, but don't let him pull you down. Make sure it's securely tied around a stable branch," Orion told them.

With the help of the brothers, they finally managed to pull the big man to safety.

Lu-onna gave the cat-woman a strange look, when she climbed back onto the surface of the tree branch. "Why did you help me? I thought you didn't like me."

"You'd do the same for me," Sheenah said.

"You're right, I would, but you didn't answer my real question." She nodded toward Whyte. "What do you see in him?"

"Nothing," Lu-onna answered. "He's paid for my services, that's all."

"Like I said," the cat-woman sneered. "You're a whore."

"I'm a companion." Lu-onna spoke calmly. "I am for hire. Some men want a whore, some men buy us for other purposes. Sometimes even women employ us. I do for money what you do for pleasure. There is no difference."

A loud crashing sound stopped their argument.

"Something's coming down," yelled Lu-onna.

They all flattened against the surface of the branch, their headlamps searching in the darkness above. Then a large object fell past, barely missing them.

"The storm must be really raging up there now," Orion commented, clinging to his branch. "We've picked a bad spot to wait it out."

"We should have stayed on the ground where we spent last night," complaint Whyte. "We would have been safe there."

"And probably drowned," Giles yelled over the howling of the wind and the splashing racket of the falling raindrops. "That little creek you bathed in this morning is most likely a raging river by now."

For the next two hours, any conversation proved nearly impossible. The rain came down in a steady stream, and even after the storm died down and the branches stopped swaying, the water kept on streaming from above.

By this time, the darkness was complete so they decided to spend the night. They unpacked their gear and pitched the tents, stringing them along the wide tree limb.

Instead of erecting her own tent, Sheenah chose to spend the night with Orion. He had already shed his wet clothing and by the faint glow of the tent light, he watched the cat-woman slip out of hers. He enjoyed the feel of dry, cool air inside the tent. The small but powerful air-conditioning coil removed the moisture and cooled down the air quite effectively, even with two people occupying the tent.

Climbing the tree and the ordeal with the storm had made Orion rather tired, but when Sheenah pressed her naked body against his, her hot kisses demanding attention, he couldn't help but respond. Her open thighs welcomed him as he slid easily into her and soon they were both hammering their hips against each other, adding their moans of ecstasy to the noise of the jungle night outside.

Satiated, they both finally fell into an exhausted slumber, from which they awoke only after Trongsan poked his blond head through the entrance and called, "Time to rise." His eyes searched the cat-woman's nude body, lingering on the fuzzy dark triangle between her slightly spread legs.

She saw his gaze but made no move to change her position. "Seen enough?" she taunted, giving him a mocking smile.

His white teeth flashed in his tanned handsome face. "It is never enough," he said with a low voice, a sly look crossing his eyes. "Maybe you'd like to change tents for a night?"

Even though the device in his necklace scrambled his thoughts, his words made clear what he meant and he sounded almost sincere, but Orion detected something else. He'd have to watch this young man with the open bright smile.

Giles had already lit a small fire on which he broiled a large snake-like animal. Where he managed to find some dry vegetation Orion couldn't guess, but the aroma of cooking meat reminded him that they hadn't eaten a descent meal since the morning before.

By the time the group started to move on, the bark underneath their feet was still wet and slippery, but with care, they managed to travel at a descent speed.

Chapter Eight

Crossing from one branch to the branch of another tree hadn't been as difficult as Orion had expected. As they traveled along the narrowing path, the smaller branches of the next tree began to entangle themselves with the one they were on, and transferring over to the wider limb proved almost a natural transaction.

Gradually the new limb grew wider until it provided them again with a solid wide and safe surface.

At noon, they stopped to take a break and to eat the rest of the broiled snake-meat.

Lying on his back, Orion studied the foliage above them. He estimated that by now they were approximately 220 meters above ground. There were still another 600 or so meters above them to the top of the trees. Not much light filtered down to this level, but he noticed leaves and lichen that glowed with their own light, creating a fairly bright environment. They didn't need their headlamps anymore during the day.

Nighttime was different. He had seen many glowing insects, but they hadn't thrown light strong enough to be useful. Even now he could see them flittering among the thicket around them. He could also hear them, a steady murmuring and whirring of their gossamer wings. Some of them were harmless, but some could inflict much harm with their venomous stings.

It seemed peaceful, but Orion knew this to be just an illusion. So far, they hadn't encountered any predators large enough to present a threat to the humans, but he knew they were there. It was only a matter of time before their first encounter.

His hand went down to his sidearm. It should prove powerful enough to take care of most of the animals they might meet. Then there were still the hunting rifles, which every member of the group carried. Except for Whyte, who had lost his during climbing, and Dr. Fortney, who left his on the ground when he decided it wouldn't benefit him to carry the extra weight.

"What are you thinking?"

Orion turned his head to look at the cat-woman crouching

beside him. She had opened to top of her suit. He could see the swell of her bare breasts through her open collar. She saw him looking and smiled.

"Tonight you can touch them again," she said, her voice low and throaty. Then she laughed. "Unless I decide to spend the night with Andrew."

"That is your choice, I guess," Orion said, a little annoyed at her assumption that it might bother him.

She pouted. "You wouldn't mind?"

He shrugged. "I don't own you and have no claim on you. Whatever you do is your decision, not mine." He smiled at her. "I would miss you, though."

She seemed satisfied with his answer, because she bent over and planted a quick kiss on his lips. "So would I," she whispered and rose.

"It's time, peoples." Giles shouted. "We still have a long way to travel."

Orion could tell by the gradual darkening that evening was near. Ahead of them, he saw the huge trunk of the tree they were approaching. He also saw the huge hole in the body of the tree. The size of the hole suggested a cave with enough room to hide a large animal…and it did.

It came rushing out of the cave, hissing angrily, spreading its short leathery wings. Before anybody could react, it swooped down on Dr. Fortney and sank its hind-claws into the scientist.

He died instantly, when the sharp nails pierced his chest.

Sheenah, whose end of her rope was tide to Dr. Fortney, reacted swiftly by unclipping it from her belt. Whyte, who was on the other end of the scientist's rope, didn't grasp the situation fast enough and was dragged along as the giant reptile tried to flap away with Dr. Fortney's body in its claws.

Lu-onna had been walking close to the merchant. When the reptile dragged him away, she threw her arms around him and clung to him, screaming. Then suddenly the rope somehow came free and they lay panting on the ground.

Almost at the same time Orion, Giles, and Zegg brought up their rifles and three bolts of concentrated energy hit the flying reptile. Mortally wounded, it fell over the edge of the branch, disappearing in the thicket below, taking the body of Dr. Fortney with it.

"You should have warned us," shouted the cat-woman accusingly. "You should have known the dangers. This is your planet."

"Easy, woman," growled the guide. "You're right. I should have been more careful, but usually the *Houn* does not attack without a warning." He approached the cave carefully. The others followed slowly, Orion closest behind the guide, his energy rifle ready. When they entered the cave, a furious hissing greeted them from the inside. The pungent, almost overpowering stench made Orion cough and gasp for air. He heard others behind him do the same.

"Young ones," Giles said. "That explains it."

Three miniature replicas of the reptile that attacked them stood on shaky hind-legs in a nest of dried vegetation, hissing and snapping at the intruders. Cracked bones and skulls littered the cave floor. Orion's practiced eye discovered a human skull among the debris, how old he couldn't tell.

"There is supper," Giles grinned and killed the animals with three short burst from his energy rifle. When he proceeded to skin one of the slain reptiles, the other members of the party protested vehemently.

"Just knowing that they may have eaten a human being, I don't think I can eat anything." Lu-onna said.

"I couldn't either," agreed Orion, and so Giles reluctantly threw the carcasses down into the forest below. "Food tablets tonight it is," he grumbled, but then his eyes lit up when he discovered a large fungus growing out of the thick bark. He went over and broke it off.

"This will do just fine," he said, his bushy mustache wiggling excitedly as he bit into the fleshy piece. "This fungus is considered a delicacy." He chewed it carefully and looked around the group who watched him with some amusement. "I suggest we sleep inside the cave tonight. It will be safer."

"In this stinking hole?" Sheenah said, wrinkling her nose.

"You won't smell it inside your tent."

They cleaned out the debris and set up their tents.

Not happy with the fungus he had eaten, Giles said to Orion, "Come on, big man, let's see if we can find something to eat outside."

They searched the thickly growing vines and leaves until they discovered one of those snake-like animals Giles had shot before. Quite a bit larger than the last one, it turned against the guide, hissing and spitting, and when he approached it, it struck out at him. However, Giles had anticipated the attack. Before the enraged animal could sink its fangs into his chest, he quickly moved aside and with a deft stroke of his hunting knife, he hacked off the grotesque head.

He chuckled and said, "Not bad for one night's work."

Orion helped him to make a fire and squatted opposite from Giles. They held pieces of the white meat speared onto a long stick, roasting them slowly and turning the stick once in awhile. The odor of the sizzling meat brought the others out of the cave. The two brothers cut a couple of thin branches growing from the juncture where the huge branch joined the main trunk and speared a few pieces of the meat.

Everyone ate and agreed it was the best meal they'd had for a long time.

After eating, when the others crawled into their tents, Orion didn't feel like sleeping, so he sat down beside the fire. Hearing someone approaching, he turned to see Zegg coming to join him.

The reptilian folded his legs under him and sat cross-legged opposite Orion. He pulled out a pack of compressed leaves and bit off a piece. He offered it to Orion. "A slight narcotic," he remarked, "it won't harm you. I know humans can digest it without discomfort."

Orion accepted it and pushed the piece into his mouth. After that, they sat silent for a while, staring into the dancing flames. He felt a little lightheaded, the result of the leaves, but it gave him a pleasant feeling. Noting Zegg staring at the ring on his finger, he said, "I usually don't wear jewelry, but this one is of some significance."

The reptilian suddenly reached into his breast pocked and removed an object, which he handed to Orion.

A ring. Identical to the one he wore.

"You're my contact," he said.

Zegg shook his head. "No, I thought you were mine."

"Peculiar," Orion muttered. "This is either some kind of ploy or there is another agent among us."

"We'll have to be careful," the reptilian said, his voice barely audible. "I guess things have gone wrong and we may not find out anything. I was watching you, because I wasn't quite sure about you, especially, since you displayed your ring so openly."

He stopped talking abruptly and Orion could feel the touch of the other's mind, questing. Carefully, he opened up his shield, letting the thoughts of the reptilian enter.

I knew you were a strong telepath, said the silent voice, *but I didn't know you were so powerful.*

Orion entered Zegg's mind now, letting the strange mind guide him. Neither of them opened up fully.

I sense you are more than just a mere telepath, came Zegg's thoughts, *there is some extraordinary power hidden inside you but I know I can trust you.*

And I will trust you, Orion sent.

There are some dark powers seeking out our kind of people. Many of our best agents have disappeared. There is great danger. This could be a trap.

Orion nodded, silently agreeing. *The same things have happened in our part of the Galactic Wheel.*

Their silent conversation was interrupted by the cat-woman, who had approached quietly. She put her arms around Orion from the back and snuggled against him. "You men sure don't talk much," she said. "Don't you have anything to say to each other?"

Orion laughed. "Sometimes you can talk without speaking."

She purred softly into his ear. "I know what you mean," she whispered. "Why don't we slip into the tent and do some of that silent talking?"

I don't trust her, came Zegg's impulses.

Don't worry about her, Orion assured him, *She is alright.*

The reptilian stood up and stretched his limbs. "It's time to retire," he said aloud. Silently he added, *I'll watch your back, brother*.

And I will watch yours, brother, Orion answered. He watched Zegg disappear into the cave and got up too. "Let's go," he said to Sheenah, "let's do some talking."

She giggled breathlessly and lifted her lips to be kissed. "Yes, let's."

Chapter Nine

Orion woke in the middle of the night to find Sheenah gone. He slightly opened up his senses, carefully searching for her mind pattern. Even her artificial mind shield couldn't suppress it completely. A strong telepath could easily find her. He detected her almost immediately, which meant she was alive and close-by. And in no danger.

He relaxed and pulled back his mind tentacles, falling asleep again. When he awoke a second time and she still wasn't beside him, he quietly crawled out of his tent. The air felt sticky inside the cave and smelled foul. At least he didn't have to worry about insects attacking his nude body, since Giles had set up a light power screen to seal off the entrance.

From one of the tents came soft whimpering sounds and harsh breathing. Through the nearly transparent material, illuminated by the faint nightlight, he could see the outlines of a female body kneeling on the floor. A man, he recognized the profile of Trongsan, loomed over her, his lean buttocks pumping with strong powerful strokes.

Orion shrugged. He had no monopoly on the cat-woman's favors. She could do as she pleased. *I guess I didn't satisfy her.* He went back to his tent, to find it occupied.

"I thought I'd visit you, since you are obviously alone."

He stared at the blond woman. "What about Whyte?"

Lu-oona lifted her shapely shoulders, shaking her long golden hair out of her eyes. "He's asleep. These last few days have been too much for him. He is exhausted, which suits me just fine."

Orion crawled under the thin blanked and lay down beside her. "Did you come to talk?" He felt her warm skin touching his.

She smiled, reached up and switched off the nightlight. He caught a glimpse of her full round breasts and pink nipples before they were plunged in darkness. Her breath came faster and her long hair fell across his face as she slid on top of him. "We can talk later, let's get to know each other better first."

Her hot breath washed across his face. It hinted of perfume

and flowery scents. His hand stroked her smooth back and moved across her fleshy buttocks, his finger gliding into the crease. He enjoyed the soft and spongy feeling of her large breasts against his chest.

Her thighs parted and with a practiced hand, she guided him into her, holding his penis while she moved slowly on top of him, teasing the head of his shaft with the thick lips of her vagina. When he was almost on the verge of coming, he felt a slight prick at the base of his organ and knew she had injected an aphrodisiac into him with one of the surgically implanted needles under her fingernails.

Lu-onna removed her hand and engulfed him completely, sucking him inside her as far as possible. He felt tiny muscles moving gently along his shaft, contracting and releasing…contracting and releasing, leaving him with an incredible sensation akin to climaxing. Yet he knew, he wasn't releasing any fluid.

"Easy, lover," she whispered, "Just lie still and give me control."

He relaxed, all feeling seemed to concentrate in his groin area and he couldn't help but moan softly. He lost all sense of time, but he knew that over an hour had passed, when Lu-onna suddenly started snapping her hips back and forth. At the same time, she dropped her mind-shield and opened herself wide.

He gasped, never expecting what he encountered when his mind merged with hers. When his sperm shot into her, their minds became one, each knowing the innermost secrets of the other one. After what seemed like an eternity, they lay panting in each other's arms. Orion stroked Lu-onna's thick, silky hair.

I would have never guessed. He laughed. *How did you know?*

She teased his bottom lip with her teeth. *I knew the first time you made love to that cat-woman. When you entered her mind, some of your energy leaked out and since I had been watching you, I picked it up. Your life force is tremendously strong, only a 'Carrier' could have such force to break through an artificial shield.*

I guess I was careless. You know about Zegg.

Yes, I know he is an agent.

They lay quiet for a while, just enjoying each other's company, when Lu-onna suddenly stirred. *I had better leave now. Whyte is starting to wake up. He'll wonder if I'm not there.*

She kissed him one last time and he felt her withdraw, leaving a feeling of emptiness behind. Then she closed her mind again. He did the same.

Before she sealed the entrance to the tent, she flashed him another smile. It wasn't the sexy smile she displayed in public but a warm and intimate gesture. "See you, brother," she whispered and disappeared.

Orion closed his eyes. It had been a long time, since he felt as content and happy the way he felt now. Not since the disappearance of his mind-sister Delina. Delina, of course, had not been like Lu-onna, who was trained in the sexual practices of a dozen races. She had been bred for sex, but only her body. The essence of her being was a completely different thing. She was a *Carrier*, like him.

Delina had been as beautiful as Lu-onna. Not quite as voluptuous, but vibrant with vitality, her life force bursting out of her. Their lovemaking had never been as intense as this one with Lu-onna, yet, the merging of their spiritual energies had reached a level just as high.

In addition, she had loved Orion as deeply as he had loved her. Remembering her brought back stabs of pain, but he still had some hope of finding her again.

A faint scraping against the entrance to the tent brought him back to the present and he opened his eyes. Sheenah slipped inside. She looked tired and worn. It had been a long night.

She saw his open eyes and smiled, stretching out beside him. She yawned and started rubbing her body against his, purring softly. "It is going to be a beautiful day," she said. "You want to start it out right?"

Orion shook his head, looking into her wide green pupils. "Don't you have enough yet?" he asked.

She pouted and gave him a sheepish look. "You know, don't you? Are you angry?"

He laughed. "We never signed any contracts. It was your idea to stay with me and if you chose to change partners, that is your privilege. I have no cause to be angry. We had some wonderful nights together and I thank you for it."

She kissed him on the nose. "Thank you for understanding. I could never stay with just one mate, but you've given me a good time." She lay back and fell asleep moments later.

Orion watched her for some time, as she mewed softly in her sleep, pointy ears twitching. She was a strange woman, very passionate and with an almost violent temper. Her sexual appetite seemed enormous. He didn't know if this was the norm for females of her kind or if she just happened to be an exception. She certainly accepted males of another species just as readily as she would one of her own kind. He wondered what the males would be like. Since he couldn't sleep any longer, he quietly dressed and left the tent. It would be daylight soon, he could see the creepers and glow-vines beginning to radiate softly, preparing for the day ahead.

When he heard subdued voices and the splashing of water coming from behind a clump of thick vines, he went to check it out and found Lu-onna and Whyte standing in a pool of water, which had collected in a deep depression. Lu-onna was scrubbing the merchant's back, her hand sneaking once in awhile around his fat stomach between his legs. The water reached just above his knees and his member jutted rigidly below his fat belly.

When Whyte saw Orion, he quickly dropped to his knees. "Can't you announce yourself?" he yelled, his face an angry red. "Or are you some kind of voyeur?"

Orion laughed good-humouredly. "You have the same thing I have," he said.

"You mean *had*," giggled Lu-onna, winking at Orion.

Whyte looked at her strangely, not understanding the meaning. Orion just grinned.

Chapter Ten

Giles made them climb up another 100 meters, since the lower branches of the tree didn't lead in the right direction. They spent the night exhausted close to the trunk of another tree. It seemed larger and taller than the others had been, because its trunk seemed immense. The next day they left, rested and eager to go on. Giles promised them that they would soon descent, but it took two more days before the branch they were on crossed the river the guide had told them would be there.

Gradually, they had descended on the previous branches, and now the river was only about thirty meters below them.

"The settlement is located on this river," Giles said. "We'll climb down here and take the river. As far as I know there are no falls or dangerous rapids along this stretch, so it should be fairly easy from now on."

It took until dark to reach the ground. They followed a narrow branch, which almost touched the ground, but in led away from the river. Giles decided to stay where they were and backtrack to the river in the morning.

Orion slept alone that night and he felt somehow grateful for that. The day had been hard and stressful and he needed the rest. Like everyone else.

Giles woke them early in the morning. After breakfast, the group headed for the river, where they spent the day building a raft from giant hollow reeds. They pitched their tents near the river. Orion spent the night alone, again, but he didn't mind. He felt rested in the morning.

It took them half the next day to finish the raft. The sun stood high in the sky when they finally shoved off.

The guide seemed pleased with himself. He sat cross-legged in the front of the raft, smoking a large, homemade pipe. Orion treaded his way carefully over to Giles, squatting down beside him. "What are you smoking there?" he asked, sniffing. "It smells awful."

Giles puffed heavily for a moment, a dark cloud of smoke

swirling around him. Then he removed the monstrous pipe and offered it to Orion. "It is an old custom from good old Earth. Try it."

"I know the custom," Orion said, declining the offer. "I've never seen much sense in it, except maybe as a ritual."

"It lets me think better," the guide said. "Because it relaxes me."

"What are you going to do, now that you've lost your plane?"

Giles shrugged. "Something will come up. I've got friends who might help me out." He squinted at Orion from under his broad brimmed hat, one eye closed. "What's it to you anyway?" he grumbled. "You people come here to hunt, looking for thrills and riches. A backwater lout like me doesn't mean anything to you. Take that cat-woman you've been fooling around with. She'd cut my throat just for the fun of it, probably getting hornier than a swamp dragon while doing it. And Whyte, that fat mud crawler, he wouldn't think twice about cutting me up with a laser. And for the rest of you…you'd watch without lifting a damned finger."

He sucked angrily on his pipe.

Orion smiled. "That was quite a speech," he said, "and you're probably right, or almost right. As for me, I have no cause to wish you harm. And I wouldn't worry about Zegg, either."

"Pah!" Giles spat into the swirling water. "To trust a *Snakeskin* is like jumping out of a plane without a grav-belt and hoping the clouds will soften your fall."

Orion lay back, laughing softly. Staring at the green sky visible between the overhanging branches, he tried to put his own thoughts in order.

He trusted Zegg fully, knowing him for what he represented. Their short mind touch had left no doubts about the reptilian in Orion's mind. He had never before met one of the reptile people and he didn't know much about them. They seemed to be closely related to the human race, since they were humanoid in appearance. They were certainly much closer to humans than the *Insectoids*, who, except for the occasional border skirmish, had no contact with the *Galactic Federation of Humans*. None of the ships that ventured into the *Hive* had ever returned, and almost nothing was known about the *Insectoids*.

A woman's pearly laughter interrupted his train of thought. He turned his head to see Lu-onna rubbing Whyte's fat belly. Whyte had removed his tight suit and was trying to sun himself in the rays of the occasional visible sun. Lu-onna giggled when Whyte reached around and put a hand over one of her fleshy breasts. She saw Orion looking and winked slyly.

Orin smiled. That voluptuous body housed a powerful spirit and behind the oversexed, silly behavior hid a cool, highly intelligent mind.

He sat up when someone called out and looked at Trongsan who pointed into the trees.

"I believe we are getting company," Trongsan said.

Orion looked at the spot Trongsan pointed at and saw tall, slim shapes launching themselves from the branches and sailing toward their raft.

"Horkas!" Giles cursed. "They're *Horkas*, the *Winged Wanderers*."

Orion watched their visitors swoop down from the trees, admiring their graceful movements. They had an enormous wingspan and they seemed to float effortlessly through the air. They came from all sides, circling the raft and calling to each other in strange, high-pitched voices.

"Are they dangerous?" Orion asked Giles and reached for his rifle.

The guide chuckled without much humor. "Dangerous and unpredictable. They are quite intelligent. I have seen them only a few times, since they usually don't come down this far south. They roam the northern part of the planet, moving constantly. Some of them live in the mountains, some in the high trees of the jungle."

He gave Orion a warning look. "Don't make any threatening moves. They carry blowguns. The darts are poisonous."

The sky above them darkened with a mass of flying Horkas.

"There must be hundreds of them," yelled the cat-woman, trying to be heard over the thunder of flapping wings.

A number of them suddenly dropped lower and landed on the raft. Some of the others kept circling, while the rest settled in the trees.

When the first one dropped onto the raft, Trongsan lifted his handgun, but Giles pushed down the young man's arm. "Don't!" he snapped, "or we'll all be dead."

The Horkas moved clumsily on the rocking raft, their leathery wings trailing behind them. They had coal black skin, but their faces were as white as bleached bones, with heavy folds of skin hanging on each side of their wide mouths. The protruding red eyes above the nose slits seemed to be in constant motion.

One of them, a tall, powerfully built brute fixed his gaze on Sheenah and then on Lu-onna. He opened his mouth, exposing a row of blood-red tiny teeth. A short gurgling sound erupted from his mouth and then he pointed at the women, issuing what sounded like an order.

Two of the others moved toward Sheenah. The cat-woman reached for the knife in her boot, but stopped when Orion squeezed her arm. "Be careful," he warned gently.

They grabbed her and pulled her toward their leader, and then they walked over to Lu-onna and pushed her also in front of the big savage. His red eyes moved back and forth between the two women, studying them. Walking around them, he looked at their backs, touched Lu-onna's long hair and felt the material of her skintight suit.

Finally, he made a motion with his small three-fingered hand, uttering a string of harsh syllables. When the women didn't move, he grabbed a piece of Lu-onna's suit, which she had slightly opened in the front, and ripped it open, exposing her breasts.

When her large breasts tumbled out there was a loud surprised sound from the others, and they came closer to get a better look. Their leader turned and called out sharply, then he reached out and ripped open Sheenah's suit. He stared at her smaller, differently shaped breasts and let his hand trail the row of her secondary breasts, twirling the long nipples between two fingers.

Sheenah hissed a warning when his hand moved across her belly and touched her fuzzy dark triangle.

The Horkas leader looked at her, showing his sharp teeth. Then he moved over to Lu-onna and opened her suit wider until her pubic area became visible. The small triangle glittered golden in the light from the sun.

The Horkas whistled shrilly, and a slim form came fluttering down from the branches to settle beside the two women.

A female.

Her four breasts jutted out sharply. They were long and thin, almost like tubes, with short, blunt nipples.

She let out a series of short high-pitched cries and strutted around the two women, thrusting out her breasts and flapping her wings. Then she stood in front of the male with spread arms and legs. Her mouth opened slightly and a long, thin tongue played across her sharp red teeth.

The male reached down between her legs and lifted a fold of skin to expose her vagina. He inserted a finger and the female emitted a soft crooning sound. He waved to one of the other males, who came closer.

The newcomer and the female spread their wings, performing a slow dance around each other, and then the female put her small hands between the male's legs, manipulating his long, thin sex-organ. In a short time his penis stood erect and, very carefully, the female guided it into the folds between her legs. The male began thrusting wildly. After a few moments, the female let out a piercing whistle and the male shuddered. Then he withdrew, his sex-organ limp and shriveling.

The couple dropped to their knees in front of their leader and kissed his clawed feet, and then they took to the air to settle in the trees.

The Horkas leader looked around at the travelers and waved to Whyte, who stood wide legged on the raft, his bare belly sticking out like a huge white balloon. When the merchant made no move to come forward, two of the Horkas grabbed his arms and dragged him over. Whyte started to resist, but one of his captors hit him across the mouth.

After the Horkas leader whistled again, another female came down to land beside him. He pointed at her and then at Whyte.

"I think he wants you to show him how you do it," Giles said sarcastically.

"Never!" protested Whyte. "Not with that ugly creature. He'll have to kill me first."

"He probably will do just that," Giles said.

One of the males holding Whyte pulled down the merchant's briefs. When the watching Horkas saw his limp but thick penis, they started to hoot, some of them coming closer to get a better look.

The female displayed her teeth, her tongue darting back and forth between them. She bent and took hold of Whyte's organ, milking it softly with her tiny hands. Whyte tried to pull back, but the two males held him tightly. When she didn't get the expected reaction, the female looked at the leader, chattering excitedly.

"You'd better get it up, lover," Sheenah said, "and I say quickly or they might just decide to bite if off."

Whyte shot her an angry look. "I can't," he whimpered, looking at Giles. "She's so damn ugly. I can't couple with an animal."

"They're not animals," the guide said.

In the meantime, Lu-onna had slowly moved to stand behind Whyte. "This will help you," she said quietly and touched his neck with one finger, injecting a fast acting drug into his bloodstream. "In a moment you will think she is the most gorgeous creature in the universe."

Whyte's mouth hung slack for a brief moment, and then suddenly his penis began to rise and he started to breathe heavily. The female Horkas was still holding his penis, her tiny hands barely reaching around it now. Whyte looked at her with glassy eyes, smiling happily. "You are so beautiful," he said, reaching for her.

Orion looked doubtfully at the merchant's pole and at the long, thin string hanging between the legs of the Horkas males. "He's going to split her wide open," he said to Giles. "Those males aren't equipped the way Whyte is."

The guide grinned hugely. "Don't worry. These females are quite adaptable."

"It seems you know what you're talking about," Sheenah said nastily.

Whyte tried desperately to push his rigid member into the female, but the standing position was not ideal because of his large belly. Finally, he lay down on his back, pulling her on top of him. Spreading her legs wide, she slowly sank down and guided his stiff mast into the folds of her sex-organ.

Giles had been right. She had no difficulty swallowing the large pole of the merchant. Holding her by her hips, he moved her up and down, moaning loudly.

Orion heard a strange popping sound and realized it came from the open mouths of the watching Horkas. They formed a circle around the pair on the ground and were making sounds in rhythm with the female's up and down movements.

She had spread wide her wings and with each down stroke she issued a high gurgling cry. Then all at once, she clamped down hard, letting out a loud triumphant wail, shuddered and collapsed on top of Whyte, who was still moving under her.

The males lifted the female gently off Whyte. When they saw his stiff penis sticking into the air they chattered excitedly. The big leader whistled again and another female came sailing down to stand beside him. To Orion she seemed younger than the first one. Her four breasts were not as large and long as the breasts of the other two females.

When she straddled the merchant awkwardly, she seemed to have some difficulty, and the Horkas leader whistled again and another female came down to join them. This was one was definitely older, because her black skin looked wrinkled and her breasts hung low, like four empty tubes. She made a few hissing sounds and reached down between the young female's legs, lifting the skin flap. Whyte pushed up with frantic movements, but couldn't penetrate the young female.

Finally, the old one pushed the younger one away and straddled the man herself. With a deft movement, she let the big penis glide into her. As soon as he had buried himself, Whyte bucked wildly under her, grabbing her thin hips and pulling her into his lap.

At first, the old female seemed to protest, but suddenly she started snapping her pelvis and pressing her legs around Whyte's thick torso. It wasn't long before she issued the same wailing cry as the first female, but she didn't collapse. With shaky legs and looking very proud, she got off Whyte, chirping weakly. She pointed at the young female, who moved again on top of Whyte. This time, she successfully impaled herself on the large organ and, moving carefully at first, she soon bounced wildly on top of the alien male, her four budding breasts bobbing up and down.

She lasted longer than the other two, and when she finally collapsed, her wailing cry was loud and triumphant. All the males cheered loudly, their wings thundering.

"She has just been initiated," Giles said. He seemed quite amused. "Sex plays an important role in their society."

"It is barbaric and vulgar," Sheenah said. "I like sex, but not as a spectacle."

It hadn't disturbed Orion. He had seen stranger things than this. "You can't judge them. It is their way of life."

Another female, also young and probably another initiate, straddled Whyte. Orion noticed that the raft had stopped moving. The Horkas had tied vines to it and anchored it to nearby branches. It looked like it was going to be a long affair.

Chapter Eleven

Over two hours had passed and Orion had counted twenty-three females who had taken the merchants rampant pole into their hairless sex-organs.

Sheenah, who had been watching with luminous eyes, said, "They'll kill him. He can't go on like that."

Lu-onna smiled. "Don't worry. The drug keeps him form ejaculating for a long time. It slows down his metabolism. But he enjoys every minute of it. There is only one drawback…when he comes out of it he won't remember any of this."

Orion noticed the cat-woman's large eyes, her breasts were rising and falling rapidly and she breathed through a slightly opened mouth. "Maybe some day you can give me some of your secrets," she said to Lu-onna. "There are possibly things I haven't experienced yet."

Whyte seemed to have come to the end of his endurance test. When the last female left him, he lay there, his organ limp.

The Horkas leader looked at Sheenah who stood closest to him, the front of her suit still open, her body exposed. His mouth opened, his teeth glinting red. Below his muscular belly, his penis stood long and stiff.

The cat-woman shrunk back, guessing what he wanted. "No way," she protested. "I'm not going to entertain the whole tribe."

"You won't have to," Giles said. "Just him."

She looked at Orion.

He shrugged. "You'd better do it, unless you want all of us to die."

Lifting her shoulders, she peeled off her suit. Naked, she lay down on the ground and opened her legs. "Com on, then," she waved to the Horkas leader who stared down at her. "Let's get it over with."

The big male pulled her up to a standing position and, with a savage thrust, pushed his thin penis into the cat-woman's organ. After a few strokes, he shuddered, roared in triumph and withdrew.

The other males cheered loudly.

On the ground, Whyte began to move and sat up, looking perplexed at his nude body. "What the hell happened?" he asked and stood up shakily. "Somebody give me some clothes, dammit!" He looked at the winged people standing on the raft. They were watching him out of red protruding eyes. "What happened to that ugly alien woman and why are they all staring at me?"

"You just fucked half the tribe's panting young virgins," laughed Sheenah. "To them you're probably some kind of god now."

Whyte looked at the others with a horrified expression. "You mean...I...that ugly creature...how?" he stammered, almost incoherent.

Orion nodded and put his hand on the fat man's shoulder. "Lu-onna drugged you. You probably saved all our lives."

Whyte shook off Orion's hand. "Why the hell me?" he asked, his voice hoarse, and glared at the others. "You should have interfered." Then he walked over to Lu-onna and hit her across the mouth. "You and your damned drugs! I hired you for my pleasure. I paid for your services and I decide what and when you do something with me. As far as I'm concerned, you're finished. I am going to make sure that not even the most degenerate lowest life form ever hires you again. You will rot on the most terrible, inhospitable prison planet I can find."

Orion saw the coldness in Lu-onna's eyes and felt the contempt she had for the merchant, but he knew she wouldn't betray herself.

"Please, Samdor," she said, her voice pleading. "I had to do it. Without the drug, you would have been unable to comply and they would have killed you. Possibly all of us. Remember, I didn't choose you. The winged people did. You know that."

"I don't know anything," he shouted. "All I know is that these bloody savages and you made a fool out of me!"

Suddenly the raft started rocking and they had to crouch down to keep from falling off. The Horkas were taking to the air, some of them pulled on the vines that were tied to the raft. It lifted into the air on one side and everybody slid into the water.

Orion felt the cool water closing over his head. He dove deeper, away from the raft, and then he surfaced. He saw the others bobbing in the water. Whyte still hung onto the raft, gasping. The air above was crowded with the flying Horkas, who were whistling and hooting, as they watched the strangers struggling in the wet element.

Their giant wings thundered when they climbed above the treetops and disappeared out of sight.

Some of the stragglers carried something. When Orion looked closer, he realized what.

Their packs with all the gear and equipment.

From now on, it was going to be a struggle to survive, because most of their weapons and protective devices were gone.

They managed to climb back onto the raft and sat without talking, each of them following their own thoughts. Darkness came swiftly, and Orion knew they couldn't just drift on in the dark.

"We should get settled for the night," he said. "On dry land."

"I don't think that would be wise. Too dangerous," Giles said, squinting ahead. "I can see a tree branch almost touching the water. We could tie the raft to it and keep it from moving. I think it would be safer."

The two twin-brothers seemed to be the least affected by the ordeal they had just been through. "We'll help," one of them said. Ross. Orion recognized him by his mustache. They stood up and waited until the raft reached the low hanging tree limb and reached up to grab it.

Orion got one of the vines that was still tied to the raft and wrapped the other end around a sturdy branch. Giles did the same with another one. "This should keep us from drifting away," he said, satisfied.

"I'm cold," the merchant complaint, sitting shivering on the wet surface.

Giles pulled himself into the thicket of the tree limb and disappeared for a while. He came back with a couple of huge leaves and threw them down. "Here, cover yourself with this," he said and disappeared again. He managed to cut enough leaves for everyone. Whyte crawled underneath his and fell asleep almost immediately, exhausted from the ordeal, his body demanding payment for the mistreatment it had received.

Orion felt pity for the merchant, a man used to being obeyed, hard and tough, not afraid to give the order to kill in cold blood. However, always backed by the products of the civilization that spawned him. There were always people around him who jumped when he commanded. Slaves. Employees. People he had bought and were afraid of him.

Now, stripped of all that, even his protective clothing with all its electronic devices, he was less then a naked savage.

If they decided to leave him behind, he would perish within a short time. He knew that and the knowledge made him angry. Worse, it drove him mad and, given the chance, he would kill to gain back his power and a measure of self-respect.

The raft rocked gently under Orion. He stared at the star speckled night sky, trying to relax. In his arms, the cat-woman stirred restlessly, crying out softly in her sleep. The air on the river was chilly and he held her naked body against his to give her warmth.

When the raft had tipped, she somehow managed to grab her boots, but her skin-suit slipped into the water, along with all the other loose articles that had been heaped in the middle of the raft.

Orion felt a soft hand touching his arm. He turned his head and looked into Lu-onna's deep-green eyes, as she squatted beside him. In the dim light of the stars, he saw her warm smile. Sensing the gently probing of her mind, he dropped his shield.

I guess the picnic is over. She kept her thought pulses at low power.

Yes, he answered, *and so far, we haven't learned anything.*

I have been wondering. Since you are not the contact, and neither is Zegg. Who is?

Orion shrugged mentally. *I think we have been sent on a wild dinosaur hunt.*

Lu-onna laughed silently. *At least you didn't lose your humor.* She almost laughed out loud, but then she became serious again.

The ring you are wearing. I have a ring like that, also, and so has Zegg. While investigating the disappearance of a high government official one of my contacts gave me this ring with the message to join the Hunt on Izzard-Junction. That's all I could get out of him. His thoughts were protected by a powerful thought scrambler. A gift from a friend, he told me. The scar behind his ear was still fresh. I wonder if we've been set up.

Well...I am not your contact and neither is Zegg. Sheenah is nothing but an adventure seeker and so is Whyte. Dr. Fortney is dead, we don't know about him. That leaves Giles, Andrew Trongsan and the two twin-brothers.

They both stayed silent for a while. *You like her,* her thought impulses said suddenly, meaning the cat-woman.

Orion smiled. *She is attractive...and available.*

But she is not human.

Neither are we. In a sense.

Her impulses changed into a higher level. *You are right, brother. Sometimes I forget. Our bodies are human, but our minds are not. The Ancient Memory makes them something alien. It alters the DNA of our bodies, makes them alien, too.*

Something stirred inside Orion's sub consciousness. From deep down, it reached up. Images of previous lifetimes flashed across his mind. The lives of his ancestors.

It is a legacy we carry, he said gently. *Each of us has a job to do. To protect the life forms in this galaxy from the Evil that has followed our ancestors from their home galaxy to this one. That Evil that creates chaos and hates other intelligent beings.*

The Evil that has hunted and destroyed the carriers of the Ancient Memory throughout the ages, Lu-onna agreed.

Orion could feel her shiver, and he knew it wasn't from the cold. A sudden sense of fear and terrible loneliness washed through her mind, spilling over to his. Her hand squeezed his arm and her thoughts cried out to let him know how much she wanted to lie in the protective circle of his arms, wanted him to caress her body, wanted his mind to merge with hers.

One of the two moons peeked through the latticework of the branches and in its meek light, he saw the glimmer of tears in her eyes.

There are so few of us, she said. *I know there are many with talents like ours. I have had a couple of lovers whose mind powers were strong, and joining with them was an absolute bliss, and yet...making love with you was like I have never loved before. The joining of our bodies is never really fulfilled without the joining of the minds. But only with another carrier can we truly merge, truly open up. With the others, even when our minds touch, we must always keep up the last barrier.*

Unless we chose to drop it, answered Orion, the memory of Delina shooting painfully into his mind.

Lu-onna picked up his thoughts and smiled. *You were lucky to find someone you could trust. Someone you truly loved. I was never that lucky. She must have been really special to earn your complete trust.*

She was. He hesitated and added. *I haven't given up hope yet. I can't believe she is dead. I won't accept that.*

If she is alive, you'll find her. Lu-onna lifted her head to look at the stars, and then she closed her eyes. *Good night, brother*, she whispered in his mind. *It is good to have you near*. She withdrew and erected the shield to keep her thoughts from broadcasting.

Orion did the same, lying awake for a long time, listening to the screams and bellows of the night creatures and the gentle sounds of the water lapping against the raft.

He thought about Lu-onna's words. The feeling of loneliness she had transmitted was nothing new to him. He lived with it every day of his life.

His body was human but the thing he carried in his mind made him different. That racial memory that was thousands of years old. That memory that told him about his very first human ancestor, Horga, a hairy savage on planet Earth, out hunting to bring food for his tribe when he encountered that strange light that had come from the stars.

These creatures seem to have large brains with a capacity for development.

Yes, my Lord, very promising.

We will choose them as hosts.

You be the first, my Lord.

Yes, we will chose the best and guide these savages in their development. However, we must be careful. The Evil Hunters have followed us across the void and they will try to destroy us. We must be careful and keep our minds closed. From now on, it will be a lonely journey for each one of us. Good-bye, brothers, sisters.

The light entered the simple mind of the savage, merged with it, changed it.

The brute had eaten from the Fruit of Knowledge.

When Horga returned to his tribe he still looked the same, but he was no longer human.

There were thousands like him on planet Earth and on other planets.

Not all hosts were human.

These chosen ones guided their fellow creatures, helped speed up their development. However, the Dark Hunters were never far away, always interfering, spreading their seeds of destruction wherever they could.

Along with their highly developed minds, the chosen ones received the gift of a long life, but they were not immortal, like the Dark Hunters.

To insure the survival of their kind they impressed their own identity into their DNA. When their bodies died, a copy of their identity lived on in the subconscious of the first-borne. Only the first-borne. From father to son, from mother to daughters, who in turn transferred it plus their own identity to the next generation.

The carriers of the Ancient Memory.

A blessing and a curse.

To be human and yet…a stranger.

People hated the different ones, feared them. They had to blend in, hide their powers. They were called witches, warlocks, devils. Orion had memories of being crucified, stoned to death, burned at the stake.

They also had been called gods, kings, heroes, priests, teachers, scientists.

The loneliness never left.

Chapter Twelve

Morning brought thick fog. It hung like a heavy curtain over the water, making it impossible to see the riverbank on either side. Even the overhanging branches of the great trees were hidden in the mist.

The travelers seemed to be alone in an endless sea of nothing.

Sheenah leaned against Orion, as they sat on the rocking raft. The current of the water had become stronger and they were traveling down the river at a faster speed than before.

"I think I'm getting a little scared," the cat-woman whispered beside Orion's ear and snuggled closer. "Floating on water has never been one of my favorite pastimes."

"There is nothing to worry about," he said but didn't actually feel that confident. He knew if they hit anything at that speed, the flimsy raft would just break apart. There would be no warning, since any object barring their way would be invisible until too late.

Whyte sat miserably in the middle of the raft, wrapped in his large leaf. "You said there are no rapids in this river, Giles," he bellowed accusingly. "If this thing moves any faster we'll…"

"Oh stop your yammering and whining," rasped the guide, interrupting Whyte. "As far as I know there are no falls. So the water moves a little faster than usual, it's no big deal. And don't blame me for the soup we're in. I didn't cook it, you did. Just keep your fat naked ass glued down and wait it out."

The merchant didn't reply. Except for his knotted jaw muscles, his face didn't show any expression.

Orion looked at the foaming water, trying to hold his position on the bucking raft. "Are you certain we're still on the river?" he asked the guide. "Look at those whitecaps. Seems to me we're already in the middle of a huge lake."

Giles grinned. "You disappoint me, Orion. I thought nothing could shake you up. Getting scared?"

Orion shook his head, smiling slightly. "I've been through worse than this, believe me. It's the women I worry about."

"The women!" Giles spat into the water. "You worry about the women? Seems to me as long as they get that throbbing piece of meat between their hot thighs they don't care where we are."

The cat-woman stiffened in Orion's arms and shot the guide an angry look, but she kept quiet.

"You have a hot tongue, Giles," Lu-onna said softly. "Be careful, or you might burn it."

The guide's bushy eyebrows went up and he stared at Lu-onna, whose green eyes flashed angrily. "Well, well," he said and chuckled. "There is another side to you. I never did believe that phony *sex-starved-dumb-female* act you've been putting on. Perhaps you can fool an idiot like Whyte but not me."

"My so-called *act* is as real as yours," Lu-onna said, a faint smile tucking on her full lips. She spoke softly, but her voice was loud enough to be heard clearly above the rushing sound of the turbulent water.

The guide shifted his position and turned toward Orion. "The river is very wide here, possibly three or four kilometers," he explained. "Actually, we are at the mouth of the river where it spills into the lake. We should arrive at our destination soon."

A sudden loud splash made everyone turn to look to one side of the raft. Something huge and gray lifted out of the water. Barely visible in the fog, but when it came closer and the travelers stared into a large, wide open mouth, displaying a double row of long teeth, they flattened as close to the raft as possible. Two black slit eyes stared for a long moment, then the grotesque head disappeared under the waves.

Orion had the impression of an enormously long and thick sinuous thing rippling in the water alongside the raft, but he couldn't be sure.

"That was a *Goark*, a giant water snake," Giles said. "They stay usually at the bottom of the lake, but one occasionally finds its way up the river. Lucky for us it didn't consider us food. They don't see that well out of the water. This one was no longer than half a kilometer, still a baby. They grow to twice that size. Fortunately, not many of them exist."

Nothing much happened for the next hour and they all sat

silent, staying close to the center of the raft, mostly lying on their bellies. Once in awhile, a wave would wash over them. Orion held Sheenah close to him, trying to keep her nude wet body from getting too cold. He could feel her shivering, but she didn't complain.

Even Whyte stayed silent. One of the waves had ripped off the large leaf he used to cover himself with and washed it overboard. He squatted naked and miserable in front of Lu-onna, who had moved closer to him to give him some protection. He didn't acknowledge her nearness, but didn't move away from her.

Finally, the fog seemed to lift and suddenly the raft stopped jumping across the waves. Almost gently now it drifted on the water. They could see the shore on one side through the patches of fog still left. Orion saw a boat tied to one of the trees lining the shore. After rounding a pile of giant rocks, they found the raft in calm, almost still water.

He saw a large beach with white sand and a number of small boats. Some of them floated in the water, tied to some kind of dock, and the rest lay in the sand.

He detected glimpses of thatched roofs between the trees.

Giles maneuvered the raft toward the beach with the only long pole that had somehow miraculously survived. As soon as they were close enough, everyone jumped off the raft and waded through the shallow water onto dry land.

The cat-woman pulled off her boots and emptied the water out of them. Then she ran barefoot through the dry sand, laughing happily. "I never thought I'd walk on solid ground again," she called back to Orion, who stood watching the trees.

He opened his senses slightly, probing the surroundings for hostile emanations. What he detected made him shout a warning, "Sheenah, come back...quickly!"

It was already too late.

Two big dark shapes came bounding out of the nearby trees, heading straight for the cat-woman.

Hounds.

Orion recognized them instantly. They came from Earth-stock, but these creatures were half-sentient. Huge mutations, their heads nearly as high as Orion. Silently, they ran toward Sheenah, who, at Orion's shout, had turned to look around.

She gave a little shriek and started to run back toward the water. One of the hounds was almost upon her, fangs gleaming dully in the half-open jaws.

Orion sent out a sharp command, directing it at both creatures. *Stop!* As if hit by an invisible barrier they both slid to a halt and looked at Orion, who walked toward them.

We mean no harm, he sent in basic symbols, keeping the paralyzing grip on their minds and bodies.

"Friend," he said aloud. "We are friends."

The hounds had no language, but they seemed to understand basic mind speech.

One of them growled, a deep rumbling sound, as Orion came closer, but then both hounds lowered their large heads and started wagging their tails. Orion reached out and padded them, sending reassuring thought.

They licked his hand, accepting him as their master.

Orion pointed at his companions. "They are friends, too," he said. The hounds growled, but without menace.

"How the hell did you manage that," Giles asked, shaking his head. "These are known as the most ferocious beasts ever imported to this planet. They have no fear and even the local predators keep away from them."

Orion smiled. "I've had dealings with them before," he said carefully. "You just have to know how to handle them. They are quite intelligent."

The guide shrugged his shoulders. "Very peculiar," he murmured to himself and looked toward the trees.

"Our welcome committee has arrived."

Chapter Thirteen

They were human. Small, slender people with olive-tainted skin and slanted dark eyes.

Orion counted nine men, all of them old, and one girl. He estimated her age around seventeen or eighteen years, Earth-standard. She looked different from the others. Her dark, slightly slanted eyes behind long, black lashes in her white face made her hauntingly beautiful. She had her thick, silky black hair tied into a loose knot.

She walked beside an old man, whose wrinkled skin was white also, but the shape of his blue eyes looked different. He was the only one with a beard. It was long and white, like his hair.

All were dressed in brown, homespun robes that reached down to their ankles.

As the girl looked at Orion with her deep dark eyes, he felt the tentative touch of a mind probe, questing, searching.

His own probe touched her gently. *Don't be afraid. We come to ask your help*. He spoke in the High Level of the Ancients.

Her eyes grew large, startled. She did not respond to the *High Sign of Greeting*, and he knew, she was not a carrier, but she had carrier blood in her, probably the second child of a carrier. She didn't know what she was, hidden here among these people. More than likely, she considered herself a freak.

Lucky he found her. She must be protected, trained, her special talents developed to the fullest.

Who are you? she asked in High Level.

A brother to you, little sister, he answered and she understood the meaning.

Smiling, she turned to the old man. "They are friends, grandfather," she said.

The old man nodded. "Welcome, then," he said.

The other men visibly relaxed and turned to walk back toward the trees. The girl walked beside Orion. She smiled at him, uncertain. One of the great hounds trotted on his other side, once in awhile licking Orion's shoulder with its long tongue.

"I am Val," the girl said aloud, but her mind touched his and a flood of questions poured into him.

She had no control. He was probably the first telepath she encountered.

Very gently, he reached out, entering her mind. She was wide open, didn't have the faintest idea how to erect a protective shield. *Easy, little sister.*

As he slipped into her mind, he could feel her shudder, almost recoiling from the intimate touch, but then she relaxed.

"I am Hektor Orion," he said, aloud.

She nodded, unable to say anything, her mind confused.

You must try to control your thoughts. Orion taught her and was surprised to see how fast she understood the principles. She had high potential and he felt elated to have found her.

You are like me, she sent, wondering, *but your mind is so…*she hesitated *…so powerful. It almost makes me afraid. I feel you could crush my mind if you wanted to.* She had managed to control the outflow of her questions, sending only what she wanted to send.

Orion sent her reassuring thoughts. *Don't worry. I could never harm you.*

They had reached the edge of the beach and walked down a narrow, worn-out path among the trees.

Then they entered the village.

Low log-houses with roofs covered by dried vegetation framed a wide, trampled dirt road. Orion saw faces of women and children peering at them through the small windows. He detected a strange sense of fear hovering over the village.

"We would like to use your communicator to call for help," Giles said, breaking the silence. "You do have one, don't you?"

"Yes, we have one," nodded the white-haired old man, "but…"

"No buts!" bellowed Whyte. "Just take us to it and get me some damn clothes!"

The old man gave Whyte a sharp look, opened his mouth to say something, but then he silently walked on.

The road ended in front of a large, dome-like building, with smooth and shiny walls. A building made from synthetic material, the only evidence that civilized people lived here. It appeared indestructible.

When one of the old men knocked against the door, it opened, revealing a clean, cool interior. Inside, a group of people faced them expectantly, fear showing in their questing eyes.

They were mostly young men and women.

The man who had opened the door said something in a strange sounding, singing language. Orion recognized it as one of the old Earth languages. The dialect had changed somewhat, but he understood most of it.

Val's grandfather answered in the same language and the young man turned away, his shoulders slumping.

Most of the others turned away, also.

"Forgive the seeming inhospitality," the old man said, "but they expected help from you and now they have been disappointed."

"Help from us?" Orion asked. "We came seeking help from *you*. Our plane was wrecked in the jungle and now we need transportation back to Izzard-Junction."

The other one shook his head sadly. "Then you are trapped. There is no way out of here."

"Where is your communicator?" rasped Giles.

Pointing to the other end of the room, the old man said, "There it is."

The group looked in horror at the smashed instrument panel. The merchant rushed over to it, his hands pulling at the melted wires and circuit boards. "What the hell is this?" he screamed, pounding his fists against the useless equipment and kicking it with his bare feet until he bled. Then he sank to the ground, sobbing. "We are stranded. No way out…" he mumbled. "No way out!"

With empty eyes, he stared into nothing. His world had finally collapsed.

One of the girls brought a robe. Lu-onna took it from her and wrapped it around Whyte's shoulders.

"I am sorry about your friend," the old man said. "He seems

to take it especially hard."

"He cracked up," Giles rasped. "Don't feel bad about it. Men like him are only secure when they are surrounded by power. Alone, they can't take the strain. They are weak and cowardly. I saw it coming."

It didn't surprise Orion to hear Giles say that. The guide was not a stupid man. He seemed to have good insights into the human psyche. "A good night's rest in safe surroundings and some food will be of help to him," he said. "For that matter, it would do all of us some good."

The girl who had brought the robe for Whyte handed another one to Sheenah, who didn't seem to be bothered by her nakedness. Orion had noticed her strutting around and the way she took enticing poses when she saw the sly glances the young men threw her.

The old man said something to the group of young people and they slowly filed through the door, along with the other old men, leaving only Val, her grandfather and the travelers behind.

"If you'd like to be the guests of my humble house," the old man said, "please, follow me. I am sure my granddaughter will be delighted to cook something for all of you." He smiled apologetically. "It may not be exactly what you are used to. We are simple people, living off the land. The soil is rich and we are rewarded for our labor. This could have been the paradise we were looking for, but even here, so far away from our home planet the devil is working his evil deeds."

He turned and walked out of the door. They followed him, pondering his words.

Chapter Fourteen

Only Zegg, Whyte and Orion stayed in the house of Val's grandfather, who had introduced himself as *Vandermar*. He was the chief of the village. Lu-onna and Sheenah went with the girl who earlier brought the robes. Giles and Andrew Trongsan stayed with another family, and the twin-brothers with another one.

Soon after eating, they put Whyte to bed. He fell into an exhausted sleep in the small spare room.

Orion, Zegg, Vandermar, and Val sat a crude table, still eating. Orion had been surprised to see the reptilian drink from the mild beverage the girl offered them. He also ate from the homemade bread and the cooked fish.

"I don't eat meat," explained Zegg, showing his pointy teeth in an apologetic smile. "My religion forbids it. But the creatures from the sea we may eat."

Vandermar still eyed the reptilian suspiciously, even though Orion assured him that Zegg could be trusted.

Val sat across from Orion. Her face looked a little flushed, as she studied him from under her dark, long lashes. She had made no more attempts to mind-speak to him, but he knew she could hardly control her emotions. He sensed her excitement and he knew that she was attracted to him. Their intimate mind touch had triggered more than just her intellectual curiosity.

He had to admit, she was a beautiful girl, no…a beautiful young woman. She had never known the love of a man before, or even felt love for a man. When her mind briefly merged with Orion's, she suddenly realized that she wasn't a freak of nature but something special. There were others like her, and some of them were males.

Intuitively she knew that she could only be truly happy with a man who was like her. A telepath.

Orion was such a man.

The old man must have noticed Val's looks, for he smiled oddly. "My granddaughter tells me that you have the *Gift*, just like she has," he said suddenly, looking sharply at him. "Is that true?"

Orion sighed. "It's true, but I wish you would keep it to yourself. What exactly do you know about Val's gift?"

Vandermar spread his long, bony fingers. "I know she can communicate with the hounds and she has the uncanny ability to know what you want to say before you say it. It doesn't bother me, I'm used to it. My wife, my daughter and Val's sister were the same way."

What happened to them?" Orion asked.

The old man looked at his wrinkled hands, and then at Orion. His old, blue eyes were moist as he spoke. "My wife was stoned to death by a group of fanatics. They said she was a witch. But she had been such a good woman, so beautiful and always trying to help wherever she could. She was a scientist and a doctor. We lived on this small, backwards planet where I was an ambassador. We tried to teach those people, tried to bring them out of the darkness, but they wouldn't let us. They were worshippers of evil, sacrificing their own children to their snake god.

After my wife's death we fled, my daughter and I. We came to Izzard-Junction and for many years, we lived in Makkuo-Tsei, the city by the ocean. There I joined the *Church of the Loving Entity* and became a minister. Our group decided one day to find our own little paradise. That's when we came here. We built this village and we were happy, at first."

"How long ago was that?" Orion asked.

Closing his eyes for a moment, the old man said, "Almost thirty Standard-years now."

"What about your daughter?"

"Oh, my daughter." Vandermar smiled, remembering. "She was a lovely child, but she grew so fast. She finally married the handsomest man of the village. And they soon had a daughter of their own. Alsie, my first grandchild." With shaky fingers, the old man combed his white beard, his eyes staring into emptiness.

"Where are they now?" Orion asked gently.

Vandermar's eyes focused on Orion and he shook his head, as if to clear his mind. He smiled sadly. "Forgive an old man for reminiscing," he said, "but I hardly have an opportunity to talk about the old days."

"Your daughter," reminded Orion, "your granddaughter Alsie and your son-in-law, where are they?"

"My son-in-law was killed by the Horkas, those winged devils. One day a whole flock of them landed in our village. They don't normally bother us, since they hardly come this far south. We are farmers, not warriors. When they tried to steal our cattle, some of our brave young men tried to fight them. The Horkas killed them all with their poisonous darts. My son-in-law was among the dead. Our boys didn't stand a chance."

"And your daughter and granddaughter?"

My daughter and Alsie were taken by slavers two years ago."

"Slavers! Here?" Zegg, who had been listening quietly, exclaimed. He glanced shortly at Orion, then back to the old man. "What did they look like?"

Vandermar stared at the reptile man.

"They were natives. Reptilians. And they all had the image of the snake god tattooed on their scaly backs." He wiped his hand across his forehead, still staring at Zegg. "As you can see I don't have much love for your kinds of people. I only tolerate you because your friend here vouches for you."

"They are not my kinds of people," Zegg said softly.

"Where they the ones who smashed your communicator?" Orion asked.

The old man nodded. "Yes. They made sure we couldn't call for help. The closest settlement is over 4,000 kilometers from here, and nothing but swamp and jungle between us. No chance of anybody getting there alive."

"What about the lake?"

"The lake stretches 3,000 kilometers to the west, almost reaching the ocean. But it would be useless. We can't build a ship large enough to take the whole village. At last count, we have 121 people living here. And if we should somehow manage to reach to ocean, then what? The only city by the ocean is Makkuo-Tsei, over 8,000 kilometers north from here. Eight thousand kilometers of rough ocean to sail. We don't have the knowledge or the manpower to build a ship that would stand the torture of an ocean voyage." He sighed deeply. "No, my friends, we are quiet alone on this planet. As far as we're concerned, we are the only living souls in the universe."

"Have they been back?" Zegg asked. "The slavers, I mean."

"Yes, they have. Twice. And we're almost due for another visit. They always take our strongest young men and our loveliest young women."

He stood up and went over to a washbasin, where he washed his hands and face. When he was finished, he emptied the water into an urn to which a hollow reed was connected at the bottom, leading outside. He pointed to a large container. "If you want to freshen up, there is clean water. Ask Val to bring you some towels. I'm going to retire, this has been a long and exciting day. I hope you have a restful night." He turned and walked into another room, closing the door behind him.

The reptilian got up and nodding toward the girl, he disappeared into the spare room.

Val looked at Orion. He smiled at her and he could see the color creeping into her face. Then he felt her mind reach out to him.

Will you sleep with me tonight? Her hand touched his gently.

You're a virgin, aren't you?" Orion asked, taking her flushed face between his hands.

I am, but you can teach me.

He kissed her lips tenderly and took her into his strong arms. "You are such a beautiful girl," he whispered into her ear, stroking her silky, black hair.

She removed the ribbon that held her hair together and shook it out, letting it spill over her shoulders. "You are so beautiful," he said again, "but also so young. I am much older than you are. I could almost be your father."

"But you're not my father," she said fiercely, stepping back, dark eyes flashing. *And I am old enough to become a woman...tonight!* she stabbed into his mind. With that, she lifted her brown robe and slipped it over her head.

She wore nothing underneath. He stared at her lovely nude body. Her skin was white and flawless, like that of a statue, her stomach flat and firm, her youthful breasts two perfect globes.

He groaned loudly when her mind caressed his and stepped into her embrace. Then he lifted her into his arms and carried her into the room she indicated.

He put her down on the narrow bed and stepped back, studying her lovely form in the flickering light of the oil lamp, while he shed his own clothing. *Like a goddess,* he thought. She smiled and then giggled, having caught his thought impulses. Her arms reached for him. *A goddess who's waiting for her god to make love to her,* she sent.

He slipped into her embrace and between her opening thighs. She cried out sharply when he took her innocence and clung to him, sobbing softly. He hushed her and stroked her face, gently kissing her lips. *The pain will go away,* he said silently. *Just relax and let it happen.*

He brought her quickly to her first orgasm and had to close her mouth with his to keep her silent. When her second climax approached, he joined his mind to hers. His strength kept her from screaming and when his own climax drew near, she tried to keep him prisoner by clamping her strong legs around his torso, bucking underneath him and whimpering like a wounded animal, but he didn't spill his seed into her, not wanting her to become pregnant. With gentle force, he withdrew, shuddering with the sudden release.

After that, she explored his body and his mind, experimenting with both. She was a good student and he taught her many things that night. Even though she was not a carrier, she had high potential, and when the night was over, he knew he loved her.

Chapter Fifteen

Orion didn't doubt that Val's grandfather guessed what had happened, but he didn't try to enter the old man's mind to find out. It was not ethical. Besides, Vandermar didn't indicate that he knew anything, so Orion didn't worry about it. At breakfast, Val sat again across from him. She looked fresh as if she had slept the whole night and she radiated such content and happiness it was almost betraying. Once in awhile her dark eyes would search his face, but she didn't try to communicate with him through her mind. Only once she smiled when he looked at her and sent, *I love you*. When they finished eating, she cleared the table, humming a little tune. Orion watched her as she moved busily about the room. The rough garment she wore hid the lovely curves of her lithe body, but couldn't hide her graceful movements. After breakfast, Vardermar told Val to show their guests around and introduce them to the other villagers, since they would be staying with them.

"You can stay in my house until you build your own," he said. "We will all help you."

Whyte slept soundly that night and he seemed to feel better in the morning, but he still walked around listlessly, keeping to himself most of the time.

Lu-onna and Sheenah joined them on their walk through the village. The two hounds sniffed around them, growling a little at first, but then they seemed to accept their presence and went back to patrolling the perimeter of the village.

"They are very good sentries," Val explained. "We have six more to guard the livestock. They keep all of the predators away, even the big lizards. We used to have more hounds, but the slavers killed them. I told them to stay away from the village when the slavers come. Their deaths would be useless, and the village needs them. Even if it means that some of us are taken away."

While they walked down the dirt-trampled road, Val hooked her left arm into Orion's, staying close to him.

Lu-onna cocked an eyebrow at him, but said nothing. Sheenah smiled crookedly and remarked, "Going after the young girls now, Orion?"

Orion smiled and shook his head. "She's old enough."

Val shot an angry look at the cat-woman. "He's not yours, and besides, you're an alien, not human. He wouldn't mate with you anyway."

Sheenah laughed. "You want to bet, little girl?"

Before it went any further, Orion patted Val's hand. "She doesn't mean any offence, Val, so don't get angry. We've been through a lot together and we are all good friends. Let's keep it that way." He looked at the cat-woman and grinned. "You don't look too comfortable in that outfit."

Sheenah pulled on the rough material of the robe she wore. "You're right, I am uncomfortable. My skin itches and I feel like taking this thing off. Like she says, I'm an alien around here. It shouldn't bother these prude people to see an alien female without clothes."

Lu-onna giggled, but became suddenly serious when she saw Trongsan coming toward them. On each side of him, hanging on his arms, walked two young women. They were laughing and squeezing his arms.

"Lovely morning," he greeted them with a wide grin.

"Looks like it has been a good night for you, too," Sheenah said, to which the young man just smiled and the two girls giggled foolishly.

"Where is Giles?" Lu-onna asked.

Trongsan shrugged. "Haven't seen him since last night. Must be busy somewhere."

The girls tucked on his sleeves and he let them pull him away. "See you later," he called and disappeared down the road.

Lu-onna shook her head. "I hope we don't run into any problems. I don't even want to know what the twins are up to. This is a very religious and close-nit group. I don't believe the older folks will appreciate it if their young daughters are taught too many new things." She looked at Orion and added mentally, *Same goes for you.*

Val looked up in surprise, putting her hand to her mouth. "You are like us," she said aloud.

Careful, warned Lu-onna, indicating the cat-woman who walked ahead of them. *Never reveal yourself to anybody unless you are absolutely certain you can trust that person completely. And even then you have to watch yourself. Yes, I am like you...and even more, like Hektor. But don't worry, I have no claim on him. I admit I am very much attracted to him, partly because we are so much alike and,* she smiled, *because he is a handsome man.*

Orion laughed out loud. *Thank you, Lu-onna. I love you, too.*

The cat-woman stopped and turned around. "I wish I had something to laugh about," she said, slipping out of her garment. "I can't stand it anymore."

They had passed the last house and were walking in a field of grass. A herd of large hoofed animals with two long horns on their heads grazed in the field. Cattle. They provided the villagers with milk and meat. Further down, they came across a field of tall grass-like plants, growing in water.

"Here we plant our rice," explained Val. "We eat the grains cooked or we bake bread with the flour. In one of our other fields, we grow corn. You probably know that corn and rice have been one of the most important foods on Earth for thousands of years. My people brought it with them when they came here. The old people say it grows better here than on Earth."

"Don't you grow any local stuff?" asked Lu-onna.

"Oh yes, we grow many different kinds of fruit and vegetables, but most of it grows wild anyway. All we have to do is harvest it." Orion listened to her talking, enjoying her soft, almost a little breathless sounding voice. She was a delight to watch and to listen to and he was glad now they met.

She must have picked up some of his thoughts, even though he had shielded them, because suddenly she turned and looked at him, smiling warmly. She reached out and grabbed his hand, pulling it toward her breast. "I am happy you are her," she said quietly. "Maybe you will find a way to get us out of here."

Very gently, he stroked her hair. "Don't put your hopes up

too high, little sister."

"A touching scene." Sheenah had been watching with interest. "He might be a man of many resources, but I'm afraid this time even he can't do much about our situation. We're all strangers on this planet, except for our guide, and he is of no help."

"Speaking of Giles," interrupted Lu-onna. "I wonder where he hides out."

"I don't like that man." The cat-woman wrinkled her nose. "There is something about him that doesn't smell right. I can't define it, but I can usually trust my instincts."

Orion knew about her instincts. She was what could be defined as a *Sensitive*. She had highly developed intuitive powers and she had learned to trust them. However, in this case, he didn't think she was right.

"Giles might not be the friendliest person around," he said, trying to defend the guide, "but I don't believe he is a bad sort." He grinned. "Just because he didn't fall for your charms is no reason not to like him."

"Pah!" Sheenah made a face at Orion. She turned and stalked back toward the village, wriggling her exposed posterior in exaggeration.

Lu-onna giggled and Orion laughed, watching the cat-woman's perfectly shaped firm buttocks move enticingly. He kept his mind-shield tightly closed, finding no sense in creating any more agitation. Women had always been one of his weaknesses. There was nothing more beautiful to look at than a nude woman, especially one built like Sheenah. Love was one thing, but sex another. He knew he loved Val, but he still loved Delina, and he was also quite fond of Lu-onna.

With Sheenah, it had never been love, she was too alien, too different, but that did not keep him from being attracted to her. Beautiful, a pleasure to look at, her lovemaking fierce and full of fire, how could he not be? He sighed. Being a man was not always easy, but sometimes quite enjoyable.

Chapter Sixteen

The raiders hit them the next day, early in the morning.

Orion slept heavily on some blankets on the floor in the spare room, after spending half the night in Val's bed, making love to her. Zegg, already dressed, aroused him from his deep sleep.

"Wake up, Orion," Zegg whispered urgently, shaking him by the shoulder. "There's going to be trouble."

Orion rubbed the sleep from his eyes. These busy nights were finally taking their toll. His body could replenish itself rather quickly because of its different metabolism, but there were limits to even his superhuman body.

He became aware of noise filtering into the room from outside and then he heard the opening of the door. Val stood there, her eyes large with fear. "They're back," she said, rushing into Orion's arms. "The slave traders are back and this time there are more than ever."

Orion dressed quickly. "Can you hide somewhere?" he asked Val.

She shook her head. "No, it's too late for that. Usually we hide inside the dome, but even that isn't always safe."

Loud noise exploded close by, someone screamed and then the door burst open. A number of tall shapes rushed into the room. They were big and fierce looking creatures. All except one were reptilian. They were naked, wearing only a small loincloth. In their large green hands, they held modern weapon. Lasers.

The non-reptilian was human. A large, heavyset man, dressed in a tight, black skin suit. A wide brimmed black hat covered his head. He didn't carry any weapons in his hands, but he had a big gun strapped to his hip.

Orion stood in front of Val, with Zegg standing beside him, his forearms held in an angle, ready to shoot his darts from under his sleeves.

The big man bared his teeth. "Looks like we have a couple of tough guys in here," he said, his voice deep and rasping. His black eyes stared with cold cruelty at them. "One move from either of you and you're all dead."

He waved to one of the reptilians. "Search!" he commanded.

The reptilian walked into the spare room. Through the open door, they could hear the noise of a scuffle and then a loud, abruptly cutoff moan. He came back out, dragging the limp body of the merchant behind him, the way a hunter would drag his downed quarry.

A pool of blood collected on the floor where he dumped the body.

Orion sensed more than saw as Val put her hand to her mouth, stifling a scream.

Whyte's throat had been cut.

The reptilian said something in a hissing language and the big man nodded. "Not much of a loss," he said in High Galact. "The fat man tried to be a hero. Lisk here didn't like that. Lisk has a bad temper." He shook his head. "Very bad temper. It's not healthy for some people." His ugly laughter echoed through the room.

Orion reached out very carefully to touch the big man's mind, recoiled when he read the filth and bloodlust and hate the other mind radiated.

That man didn't need an artificial thought scrambler, he had something much better than that. No telepath in his right mind would try to enter that mess. Orion realized, here was a very dangerous man and he sent a tight beam at Zegg. *Caution*!

He tried to contact Lu-onna and encountered her familiar pattern immediately.

What's happening out there, sister? he asked.

We've been captured, she sent back, relaying a visual image with her reply. When he 'saw' the large number of raiders, he knew there was no sense to resist. It would cause only unnecessary deaths.

"Alright," he said. "We'll come peacefully."

He put his arm around Val. "She stays with me."

The big man shrugged and turned to leave. They followed without another word.

A cold shiver ran down Orion's spine, when he looked at the

naked backs of the natives. Tattooed between their shoulder blades writhed the image of a serpent.

Outside, Orion saw with his own eyes what Lu-onna had transferred to his mind. There were at least twenty or thirty of the reptilian natives rounding up the villagers. Most of them sat on huge long-necked armored creatures with long, flat heads and rows of sharp teeth. He counted a dozen humans among the raiders. They floated above the scene in one-man gliders, watching the natives gather up the prisoners.

Orion found Val's grandfather lying in the dirt on the street, unmoving. He looked dead, but after probing carefully, Orion detected faint pulses coming from his brain. He was just unconscious and would recover. Val cried out when she saw the old man, but Orion held her back.

He's alive, he said. *Leave him be, he'll be safe.*

The raiders separated the young people from the old ones and the young children.

Orion counted fourteen young women and twelve young men, who were herded to one side. The reptilians ripped the robes off their bodies, tied their hands and feet and then carried the naked prisoners to their mounts and laid them across the wide backs of the beasts.

Lu-onna and Sheenah stood to one side, waiting for Orion and his party. Four savage looking brutes were covering them with lasers.

One of the natives approached the Cat-woman and reached out to pull the robe off her. She moved back, out of reach, grabbed the hem of the robe and pulled it over her head. Except for her boots, she was naked.

"Don't touch me!" she hissed.

Somebody laughed.

"She's a hell-cat, that one," said a familiar voice.

Orion looked around, astonished. His eyes fell on the speaker. There, beside a couple of the human raiders, stood Andrew Trongsan, a big smile on his face, and behind them, a satisfied looking man with a wide-brimmed hat and a big, bushy mustache...their guide.

"She needs a good thrashing," grumbled Giles, "or a knife across the throat."

Sheenah turned and looked at them. "So you two are part of this bunch of cutthroats. You never liked me, Giles, but you...?" She stared at Trongsan. "I realize you didn't love me, Andrew. Things between us were purely physical, but would you really let these animals touch me?"

Trongsan just grinned and shrugged his shoulders. "What do I care what happens to you. You gave me a good fuck, but there are lots of other willing cunts. Some of them are even human."

One of the two humans beside him grinned, rubbing his crotch. "I haven't had a good lay for ages. Do you think she could handle me, Andrew?"

Trongsan laughed. "Can *you* handle *her*? She's got a voracious appetite."

The other one advanced toward the cat-woman, who watched him warily. His hand reached out to touch her breast.

Things happened so fast, even Orion hadn't been able to follow it closely. Before the raider's hand touched her, Sheenah stepped back, her hands grabbed his arm, and turning, she threw him across her shoulder. He sailed through the air and crashed to the ground some distance away behind her.

She was fast, Orion had to admit, and incredibly strong.

The raider cried out in pain and stood up, groaning. He slowly advanced toward the woman, an ugly expression on his face. "Nobody makes a fool out of me and gets away with it," he growled. "I'm going to cut you good, bitch!" He pulled a big knife from its sheath on his belt and waved it in front of him.

Sheenah waited for him, her hands hanging limply on her sides. Breathing through her slightly open mouth, she displayed sharp teeth behind curled-up lips.

Close now, the raider stabbed at her chest, but she stepped aside with a fluid movement, her hand dipped to her boot and with her left, she thrust his knife arm away. Her right hand came up, described a short arc and her attacker fell back, a gurgling sound issuing from his throat.

His hands flew up to his neck, trying to stop the blood from gushing out, but his throat had been cut from one ear to the other.

"I've entertained a whole tribe of sex-crazed voyeurs. That was enough. From now on…anybody wants a piece of tail, I'm not available!"

Her attacker had fallen to the ground, his legs kicking. Then he lay still, his face in a pool of blood.

"He's dead!" shouted the one beside Trongsan. "She's killed him, the bitch!" He lifted his laser and pushed the firing stud, burning the spot where the cat-woman had been standing. The moment he lifted his weapon, Sheenah dropped and rolled away. The raider cursed, moving his laser, but the cat-woman kept rolling toward him.

Still on the ground, her hand flipped back and shot forward. Her assailant's curse stopped in mid-sentence. He dropped his weapon, his hands clutching the hilt of the knife protruding from his chest.

Before anyone realized what had happened, Sheenah moved in, grasped the knife and pulled it out of his chest. The lifeless body of the raider collapsed to the ground. She bent down to wipe her weapon on his coat.

When she looked up, her eyes were large and bright. Very casually, she picked up the fallen laser and, as if by accident, she pointed it at Giles. "Anybody else wants to try?" she asked, almost gently, but Orion detected the tension in her voice. He knew none of the raiders would come close to her without her consent. He would die fast. However, he saw several lasers trained at Sheenah and he braced himself to the sight of her charred body falling to the ground.

"This has gone far enough," bellowed a voice. "No more killings!" The big outlaw leader stared coldly at the cat-woman. "You can put your weapon down and live or you keep it and be blown to bits. Either way…I don't care. Should you decide to live, I promise you, no one is going to touch you as long as I'm in charge."

He turned to Giles. "Where the hell did you pick her up? I thought we had agreed to handle only humans?"

The guide shrugged. "She looked human enough to me. I

couldn't very well turn her down if I let that reptilian come along. The party is small enough as it is. We've lost three of our members already."

"Yeah," Trongsan agreed. "Not much profit this time, especially since we lost the plane."

"Don't worry about the damn plane. We'll get you another one." The big man looked thoughtfully at the cat-woman. "We can count ourselves lucky this one's a female. If you think the local natives are savages, you'd find them harmless if you ever encounter her male counterparts. Two of them would wipe us out and they'd enjoy doing it." He lifted his arm. "Now, let's get moving."

Sheenah put down her laser. Nobody seemed to take notice when she casually sheathed the knife in her boot.

A large skimmer landed in a cleared area and their captors ordered Orion and his party to board it. The leader and a few guards took their places inside and they lifted off. Giles and Trongsan were not among them, but Orion had seen them take the one-man gliders of the two dead raiders.

The wailing of the old people who had been left behind echoed still in Orion's ears. He padded Val's hand. She pressed herself against him, her face pale.

Don't worry, little one, somehow we'll get out of this.

Lu-onna, who must have been tuned in to him, carefully entered his mind on a very high, almost undetectable waveband. Even if Val were connected to Orion, she wouldn't be able to listen in.

We're getting closer, brother. Did you see?

Yes, sister, Orion answered, *I saw. The sign of the Scaly-One.*

He looked at her, smiling faintly. The silly, dumb-oversexed-vixen image had left her face. Still beautiful and extremely attractive, the expression of her eyes had changed. No more large and innocent, now they were watchful and cool, almost cold, matching the intelligent mind hiding inside her beautiful head.

Lu-onna knew his thoughts and smiled. Then she nodded and that hard glint in her eyes vanished.

Chapter Seventeen

Orion estimated that no more than an hour passed before they landed. The skimmer set down alongside a large building, built entirely from stone. Its strange design made it look out of place among the huts surrounding it.

Two giant serpents hewn out of stone writhed around the pillars holding up the canopy to the entrance.

Lu-onna glanced at Orion, who nodded grimly.

A place of worship, he sent.

They were directed toward a small log building, obviously their prison. Before they entered it, they were ordered to disrobe. Reluctantly, Orion undressed, throwing his clothing on top of the pile the others had already made.

The cat-woman, already nude, pretended not to hear, but after being prodded in the back with a laser, she removed her boots. She tried to palm the knife, without success, and threw it on top of the pile, growling angrily.

Seeing Zegg for the first time without clothes, Orion marveled at the sleek, muscular body of the reptilian. The lack of a scrotum between Zegg's legs looked odd, made him look like a neuter, but Orion knew better.

After slipping out of her robe, Val moved close to Orion. Her face looked flushed, and she shamefully tried to cover her young breasts with one arm and her pubic area with the other.

Lu-onna drew a few stares from the human guards, but they said nothing.

"Don't entertain any ideas of trying to escape," warned the outlaw leader. "Even if you should manage to slip by my guards, there is nowhere to go. There is nothing but swamps and impenetrable jungle all around us." He chuckled gleefully. "And there is no Giles to guide you. He is the only one who might be able to lead you to safety, but he is on my side."

He turned and walked away, into the stone building. The guards motioned them to go inside the log-house, and without much enthusiasm, the group followed their orders.

The log-house consisted of one single room, devoid of any furnishings. The floor was nothing but trampled dirt.

The rest of the prisoners arrived in late in the afternoon. After having their bonds removed, they were also herded into the cabin, which suddenly seemed small and crowded.

Most of them presented a sorry sight, their bodies filthy and scratched up from their journey on the backs of the giant reptiles.

When night came, they all lay down on the hard dirt floor, trying to catch some sleep and rest up for the next day.

Val snuggled into Orion's arms. "What's going to happen to us, Hektor?"

"I don't know, little one." He hugged her tightly. "We'll have to wait and see. Get some sleep now."

He didn't sleep soundly. In his arms, Val moaned once in awhile, as if trapped in some nightmare. Awaking from it wouldn't bring any relief.

By morning, the air in the cabin reeked of unwashed bodies and the sweat of fear. Orion woke early. Gently removing Val's arms from around his neck, he rose and stepped over the still sleeping bodies to get to the door. It didn't surprise him to find it unlocked.

Outside, two guards sat sleepily on either side of the door, weapons across their knees. They barely looked at him when he walked by them, but he knew they were watching.

He looked around to find a place where he could answer nature's call, when someone else stepped out of another log-house.

Giles.

When he saw Orion, he came toward him, smiling. "You're up early," he said with his rasping voice. "Sorry, things turned out this way. I rather took a liking to you."

Orion felt a bit uncomfortable standing in the nude in front of Giles, who still wore his outfit. "Why?" he asked. "Why are you doing this?"

The guide shrugged, puffing on his pipe. "Money. It's good business."

"What happens to all the people you bring here?"

"They get shipped off-planet. I don't know where they end up, and frankly, I don't care. Most of them are drifters and adventures, seeking fortunes. Nobody misses them." He looked at Orion with narrow eyes. "You're different from most of the riff-raff I take on these hunting trips. Too bad, but I have no choice. I don't work alone. Maybe you'll get lucky…you're a survivor."

He tipped his wide brimmed hat and turned to go. "Good luck."

Orion looked after him.

Strange man. He shook his head. *Strange, and with few scruples.*

* * * *

The day went by without much happening. They were free to walk around the camp, but were stopped when they tried to enter the temple. Orion saw more prisoners in other log-houses. He saw several more groups of hunters, most of them human, or at least humanoid.

Like Giles said, the majority of prisoners were drifters, people nobody would miss. When Orion talked to them, he found out that one group had been there for twenty days already, and he knew something was going to happen soon.

That night all of the prisoners were herded into the temple. Everyone had to stand, because there were no seats.

The place was filled to capacity.

The prisoners, Orion estimated about 150 of them, stood in the front, close to a raised platform…a stage. Behind and around them, stood the natives, their lidless reptilian eyes glittering as they stared at the dais.

The inside walls of the temple were covered with crude drawings, depicting scenes with huge reptiles, natives with long necks and snake-like beasts. Statues of lizard-like beings, carved from stone and wood, crowded around the statue of a giant snake.

Orion shuddered as he studied the giant statue. He had never liked snakes.

A ghostly voice whispered inside him and he pushed it aside. His mind reached for Lu-onna and she welcomed his touch. Her thoughts were sober and he sensed her inner turmoil.

We are near, brother, she said and he withdrew.

A fire inside a large bowl in the back of the dais, the only source of light in the huge temple, lit up the dark with an eerie flickering light.

The sound of drums interrupted the silence and as if from out of nowhere a figure appeared in the center of the dais, standing unmoving like a statue, while regarding the prisoners and assembled worshippers with large, black protruding eyes.

From the figure's shoulders hung a black cape, covering the body underneath. Only the head was visible. The head of a serpent.

From behind a curtain, two more figures rushed out silently, natives, probably some kind of acolyte. They also wore black capes.

Then from the other side came two more, between them they lead another. A human male. He was young, his nude body reflected the flickering light, his smooth skin shiny, covered with oil.

He stared straight ahead, as if in a trance, a dreamy smile on his face.

Drugged. There was no doubt in Orion's mind.

The drumming became louder. He became aware of a strange hissing sound and, looking around, he saw the natives slowly weaving back and forth, while emitting that eerie sound.

The silent figure in the center of the dais began to stir. Then with one quick movement, the cape was flung aside, revealing the naked body of a woman. Her black skin shimmered with iridescent colors. Her breasts were large and strutting and her buttocks round and quivering as she moved toward the young man.

Her body moved sinuously, sometimes slow, sometimes impossibly fast, as she began to dance. She seemed to be without bones, bending her body into positions a human body could never attain.

The young man seemed to watch her in fascination. She rushed up to him and touched his body, but when he reached for her, she pulled back, eluding him.

The drums stopped abruptly, the natives stopped chanting. Moving slowly toward the young man, the female put her hands around his erect member and, bending backwards, she guided the throbbing penis into her vagina.

Very slowly at first, her body undulated, picked up speed as the drums and the chanting began again. After entering the woman's sex-organ, the young man started thrusting, but the acolytes held his hips, so he just stood there, an expression of rapture on his face.

The way the female figure moved her body, Orion had the strange sensation, he was watching a serpent playing with its victim.

The man shuddered and a soft moan escaped his lips. The female pulled back suddenly, releasing the spurting organ and, with a fluid movement, she took it into her open mouth.

A knife had appeared in one of the acolyte's hand. He plunged it into the young man's throat. The other acolyte collected the flowing blood into a large vessel. The rolling of the drums and the ecstatic chanting of the natives swallowed up the gurgling scream of the dying man.

Orion felt a wave of nausea overcoming the watching humans. Val, who stood beside him, gripped his arm tightly.

"It's horrible," she cried out. "They just murdered him."

Orion hugged her to him. *There was nothing we could do*, he said in mind-speech. *I'm sorry.*

The acolytes on the stage passed the cup, and each one drank deeply from the blood. Then they knelt down in front of the rigidly standing female. She stood, her arms held high and her legs spread wide. Each of the acolytes moved between her legs and with their long tongues, they thrust into her vagina.

After they were finished, the female uttered a piercing cry. Her reptilian eyes looked over the humans. With one long finger, she pointed. Two acolytes followed her pointing finger. They approached Orion and Val, who stood close to the dais.

They reached for Val.

Orion moved in front of Val, his eyes cold and his face hard. "No!" he said fiercely. "Nobody touches her!"

One of the acolytes brandished a long knife, thrust it at Orion's midriff. He blocked the knife arm with his left, his right fist smashed into his attacker's face. Hearing bones crack, he turned and kicked the other one in the chest, sending him sprawling.

Other acolytes rushed in, but suddenly there were three people on the platform, blocking them...Zegg, Lu-onna, and Sheenah.

A loud hissing cry stopped the attacking acolytes. The female held up her hand and said in High Galact, "Get back. None will be harmed." Her cold glittering eyes lingered on Orion, and then she turned and disappeared behind a curtain.

"Too bad," Sheenah said, "I was looking forward to a good fight. There hasn't been any action for awhile."

Val looked at Orion with large eyes. "Thank you," she whispered and, in mind speech, she added: *I love you.*

He smiled and pulled her close.

Chapter Eighteen

They had already bedded down, when the door opened and two human guards entered. Searching the sleepers on the floor, one of them waved to Orion.

"You!" he said. "You are wanted. Come!"

Val reached for his hand. He squeezed it. *Don't worry, little sister. I'll be back.*

The guards led him into the jungle. Stopping in front of a log-house, one of them ordered, "Inside!"

He pushed open the door and, carefully, he stepped into the cabin. His mind searched, sensing the presence of someone in the room, behind a curtain at the back. His probe encountered nothing…no barrier, no artificial shield…nothing. According to his searching mind tentacle, nobody was there, but he knew someone was.

"Close the door," came a familiar voice.

He stayed close to the door, waiting.

"Come closer. Don't be afraid."

The torches on the walls flickered as he walked past them. He parted the curtain.

She stood in the middle of the other room, her voluptuous naked body silhouetted against the pale light of the moon flooding through the window.

She had her back to him.

"The moon shines bright tonight," she whispered. "Almost as bright as on my home world."

She turned and Orion suppressed a sound of surprise.

"I hope you're not disappointed." Smiling, she came closer, her hips swaying smoothly.

Orion felt a strange attraction toward her. He tried to read her mind, but there was nothing there. He finally understood.

She was a mute. A *mind-mute*.

She let the moonlight fall on her face. Her eyes reflected the light in many colors and her white teeth looked like a row of pearls inside her slightly open mouth.

Her face was human and lovely.

Seeing the look in his face, she laughed. "It was only a mask. I am their *Serpent-goddess*, you know. So I have to look like one."

Turning slowly in front of him, she asked, "Do you find me attractive?"

"You are beautiful," Orion answered and reached out to touch her naked shoulder. It felt smooth and warm.

She moved closer, her breasts grazing his chest. A shiver ran down his spine and he stroked her back. He felt compelled to bend down and kiss her full lips, when she suddenly pushed him away, laughing.

"You do find me attractive," she murmured, looking him up and down. "You are a fine specimen of a male. I think we may enjoy each other for a while. Would you like me to dance for you?"

Finding himself unable to speak, he just nodded.

Her eyes stabbed like fiery flames into his mind. Slowly her body began to undulate, her hips moved seductively and he stared in fascination at the hairless puffed mound below her flat belly. He didn't see a navel, only smooth skin. Faster and faster, she twirled in front of him, around him. Bending backwards, her round skull touching the ground, she pushed up her vulva.

Opening and closing her shapely thighs, she presented the fleshy lips of her sex-organ, letting him see the pink inside, and he couldn't help but react.

Rising, she took his hand and pulled him toward a pile of pillows. "Come," she whispered, sinking into the soft mountain. "Lie down beside me."

He couldn't resist and followed the pull of her hand. She pressed herself against him, her body soft and warm and he groaned when her hand took hold of his rigid member.

"I like what I feel," she murmured, nibbling his ear. Gently she pushed him onto his back. Then she sat up, straddled him and slowly she fed his throbbing shaft inside her alien vagina.

He watched the smooth, thick lips close over his manhood and the liquid softness he found inside her almost brought on an instant climax. He controlled the urge and watched as she slowly rotated her hips.

Maybe she had chosen this spot deliberately, maybe it was just pure chance. The light of the moon bathed her body fully and her black skin seemed to shimmer with a soft iridescent glow. He could make out the tiny scales covering her skin and it confirmed her reptilian ancestry.

She watched him from under half-closed lids as her body adopted a different rhythm. Suddenly, he had the illusion of a giant serpent undulating above him. Her body swayed back and fort...back and forth...Her strange eyes were wide open now and held his gaze. He reached out, his hands closing over her full breasts, stroking the thick nipples.

She can't be reptilian. She has breasts.

Almost on the verge of coming, he tried to hold back. He didn't want it to end yet...not yet. It felt so incredibly good.

"You're doing fine," she breathed, her hands gliding over his chest.

He wanted to push up, enter her deeper, but her weight held him down, her strong thighs clamped around him like a vice, keeping him immobile.

Her eyes burned into his. "Now!" she said. "Now!"

He let go, climaxing inside her. When the intense wave of pleasure hit him, he shouted hoarsely. He hardly felt the slight stinging sensation around his penis.

He climaxed...and climaxed, felt the liquid pumping out of him into her.

"Good," she whispered. "It feels so good."

From deep inside him, something protested.

Stop her! Danger!

But it felt so wonderful.

When the climaxing didn't stop, he suddenly knew what she did.

She was feeding.

Tiny suction cups inside her vagina were sucking the blood from his penis, but he didn't care. Why fight something that made him feel so glorious?

His eyes were on her face. He mouth stood open, a long forked tongue played across her pearly teeth and she emitted a soft hissing sound. Her black serpentine body rocked back and forth and he kept his hands clasped on her lovely breasts.

When it was finally over, she stretched out on top of him, kissing him on the mouth. "You are good," she said between kisses. "Very good. I am satiated."

After a while, she slid off him and lay back. "You know what I did, don't you?" she asked.

Orion yawned, his eyelids heavy. To speak seemed such an effort. "You sucked my blood," he murmured. "But that's alright. I was in no danger." He remembered now. He had run into her kind before, in another lifetime, a long time ago.

They had called her a witch. She lived alone in the forest, a beautiful black woman from a distant land. The men from the nearby villages had been drawn to her like moths to the flame. They whispered of the strange rites she performed and of the heavenly pleasure she gave those who succumbed to her charms.

Until finally the angry women of the villages banded together and burned down her hut with her inside.

The women called her *Satan's Bride*, to the men she had been a *Goddess of Love*.

* * * *

When he awoke the light of dawn spilled through the window. He found the woman bent over him, her long split tongue teasing the tip of his penis. "You're awake," she said, smiling, and proceeded to swallow his now erect shaft. After a short time when he felt the pressure mounting, she let go and slid up his body.

Orion put his hands on her arms and pushed her into the pillows, then he moved on top of her,

"This time we do it my way," he said.

She just laughed softly, opened her legs wide and let him enter. Again, he experienced the same incredible softness inside her and it didn't take long until he was ready to shoot his semen into her. As soon as he let himself go, she wrapped her legs around his buttocks, pressing him to her and making it impossible for him to move. At the same time, he became aware of the tiny suction cups drawing blood from his spurting member.

This time she kept her eyes closed and moaned loudly. She released him soon and he withdrew gently. Opening her eyes, she gave him a warm smile. "You gave yourself freely this time. It is very unusual."

"Like I told you last night, I knew I wasn't in any danger," he said, lay back and relaxed. "Tell me, do you enjoy it as much as I do?"

She laughed. "Do you enjoy eating?" she asked.

"Of course I do, but I wouldn't exactly call this eating."

"For my species it is a form of taking nourishment. It is very pleasant."

"Is that the only way you keep yourself alive?"

Her hand slid over his massive chest. Sitting up, her iridescent eyes regarded him for a while, then she shrugged. "No, of course not. We eat the same way other creatures do, only once in awhile we have to have some blood."

"How about your men? What do they do?"

"Men? You mean males? There are none. We are of one sex."

Raising his eyebrows, Orion asked, "How do you propagate?"

"We use the sperm of other males…like yours, for instance."

"But our species is not compatible?"

"It works, believe me. Once a season we lay two or three eggs, if they've been fertilized and if we want young we let them hatch. If we don't want any offspring, we eat the eggs." She laughed. "Usually I eat them."

Orion shook his head in disbelief. "Obviously you need human males. What if there are no human males around?"

She laughed again, stretching languidly. "Any male will do, but I prefer the human kind." She kissed him. "You gave me much pleasure and I like you. I may just decide to hatch your egg."

"I don't understand one thing. Since you are laying eggs, that means you are not a mammal and yet…you have breasts with nipples. What are they for?"

Her tongue flicked over his lips. "You sure ask a lot of

questions," she murmured. "I don't have all the answers. My race developed on a planet where we had to compete with another species: Humans. Since we had to attract human males to ensure our survival, nature gave us certain attractive traits, including the human female form." She stood up and stretched, looking down at him, a curious smile playing over her lips. "You told me that you found me beautiful."

"I meant it. You *are* beautiful," Orion said, his eyes feasting on her lovely form. In the daylight, she looked even lovelier and very human. The fact that she was completely bald only seemed to enhance her attractiveness.

He closed his eyes for a moment. Another woman he felt attracted to, this one even more alien than the cat-woman. It disturbed him, especially since she represented something he had come to hate and fear.

Opening his eyes, he saw her looking at him, still smiling. "Who is the Serpent-God?" he asked.

"He is the Serpent-God," she said and turned away. "You will not want to meet him." When she turned around, her smile had vanished.

"Go now!"

Chapter Nineteen

A large trans-space freighter landed in the afternoon that day and all the prisoners were herded aboard. Hours later, they felt the spaceship land and soon guards appeared and commanded them out.

"Where are we?" Val asked Orion.

"We must be on one of the moons," Orion said.

His assumption was confirmed when they left the ship. It had landed beside a huge bubble. A transparent tunnel connected the ship to the bubble.

The young people were not used to the lighter gravity of the moon and were staggering and bumping into each other.

Once inside the bubble, they encountered a number of flat buildings, square and ugly, like army barracks. The prisoners were driven into the largest building, where a tall baldheaded man met them. He stood on top of a raised platform, dressed in black, his dark eyes regarding the prisoners silently.

On the front of his black tight fitting uniform, he displayed the image of the writhing serpent.

Carefully, Orion reached out with his mind, but his mental finger touched only a strong mind-shield.

Very strong and natural.

As soon as she touched the barrier, the black eyes of the tall man searched him out. He said nothing, but Orion knew the other one had sensed his probe.

The bald man looked over the assembled prisoners and gave them a dry smile.

"I guess you're all wondering what's going to happen to you? Forget about ever going home again. You will take a long trip. You will cross from this arm of the Galaxy to the next. You're not the first ones. Many have been taken across already to colonize the next spiral arm."

He laughed cruelly. "You're colonists. One thing though…you're no longer free. You've been sold to our friendly neighbors. From now on you are slaves." He made a gesture toward the back. "Meet your new masters."

From one of the entrances in the back stepped four creatures. Their black multifaceted eyes glittered under the bright overhead lights.

Insectoids.

Lu-onna, who stood close to Orion, touched his mind. *There is our answer. Now we know what happened to the kidnapped people.*

You are right, Orion sent back sadly. All hopes of ever finding his Delina were dashed. However, there was a bright side to this. She was probably still alive, even though many light years away.

He looked over the frightened faces of the others and felt sorry for them. Some of them started to cry, others shouted defiantly.

The bald man lifted his hand. "You have no choice, so you might as well accept it. You won't be treated badly, unless you disobey. Tonight you'll stay in your assigned quarters. Tomorrow you will be transported to the big ship that will take you across the gulf. It's a long journey. Have a good trip." He waved, threw back his head and laughed.

Anger welled up inside Orion and he felt like jumping on the platform and smashing his fist into the bald man's cruel face. The man responsible for his mind-sister's disappearance.

Lu-onna sensed his turmoil and gently she laid a hand on his arm. *Easy, brother. We'll have to wait until we can act.*

He squeezed her hand. *You are right, sister. Now is not the time. Thank you.*

The guards divided them into groups and they were distributed among the buildings where they met other prisoners. Orion's group was the last batch of slaves to arrive before the *Big Jump.*

Humans and non-humans alike, all of them were scared. Nobody knew what exactly lay ahead. There were rumors that some of the Insectoids used slaves to raise their young. They deposited their eggs into a slave's body, where they hatched and grew, slowly consuming the host body from the inside.

The rooms they were in were large, but with so many prisoners, they filled up quickly. At least they had adequate toilet facilities. Their captors didn't want the rooms messed up with feces and other waste products.

Before they entered the rooms, they had to pass through a decontamination chamber, where they were bathed with cleansing rays.

Guards, displaying heavy weapons, lined the corridors, and Orion questioned the reason. Even if the prisoners decided to break free, where would they go? Naked and unarmed, they were stranded on a hostile, airless world. The only protection the dome above the buildings.

At sleep-time, the lights in the rooms dimmed to allow the slaves to sleep. Only the lights in the corridors were brightly lit.

Lying on his cot, pretending to sleep, Orion send out a searching mind probe. There were only four guards in the immediate vicinity and they didn't appear very alert. His mind found Zegg. *Want to go exploring?*

The reptilian had been doing his own searching. He gave Orion an affirmative and carefully they left their places. Lu-onna and Val were already sleeping, only the cat-woman stirred, when they walked silently past her.

Orion laid a hand over her mouth. "Be quiet," he whispered. "Zegg and I are going to have a look around."

She wanted to come along, but he convinced her to stay.

"Males!" she protested. "Always want to be heroes."

Orion smiled and gave her a quick kiss. "We don't plan to do any heroic things."

Luckily, their room was close to the main entrance and slipping past the guards proved easy. The doors were open and Orion's probing detected no presence outside. The buildings lay in darkness, only a few lights lit up the inside of the huge dome.

"I saw a hangar-like building when we came into the dome, close to the main airlock," Orion whispered.

Zegg nodded. "I saw it also."

Keeping their minds open, they headed in the direction of the lock. They found the building and carefully they entered it to find themselves inside a small room.

"This is an airlock," Orion said and checked the gauges on the back wall. "There is air in the building." He tried to open the heavy door and didn't encounter any resistance.

Inside the building stood a small space shuttle. The airlock above it was sealed.

"This could take us back to Izzard-Junction," Zegg said.

"Yes, it could," agreed Orion. "There is only one problem. Should we be able to get out of the airlock undetected, once we lift those fighters I saw outside will shoot us down before we even leave the gravity of the moon."

Zegg emitted a hissing sound. "I've thought of that too. In other words…this craft is useless to us."

"I'm afraid that is so."

Both of jumped and looked around for some place to hide when searchlights flared up suddenly, throwing their shadows against the wall behind them.

"Stay where you are! Don't move!" a sharp voice ordered from speakers above them.

They tried to run anyway, but a bolt from a hidden stunner stopped them in their tracks. Zegg went down. Orion absorbed the shock, but he let himself slide to the ground. He lay quiet, waiting. He felt the pain of the energy bolt that had hit him, but he was conscious.

A few minutes later two guards came through the airlock to the hangar. Orion watched them come closer.

One of the guards looked at him. "Hey, this one has his eyes open," he called to the other guard. He gave Orion a hard kick. Orion grabbed his foot and twisted. The guard fell, drawing his gun while trying to keep his balance. Before he hit the ground, he managed to pull the trigger. Again, Orion tried to absorb the energy. The jolt had been at close range and his muscles jerked from the pain.

He closed his eyes to concentrate on the pain and realized he had made a mistake. He could hear the voice of the other guard as he spoke to somebody else.

"Sorry to bother you, commander. We've caught two of them

inside the hangar hanging around the shuttle."

"So take them back to their quarters. I have not time to bother with escaped slaves."

Orion recognized the voice. It belonged to the baldheaded man who had welcomed them.

"There is something strange about these guys. The reptilian is out cold, but the other one, he's still conscious. He's pretending to be out, but the detectors show he's not. He's been hit twice."

"Well, alright, bring him then."

Orion received another kick between the ribs.

"You! Get up!"

He stopped pretending to be unconscious and stood up, holding his chest. "Did you have to kick so hard?" he complained.

The guard he had thrown to the ground hit him across the face with the back of his hand. "Shut up!" he growled and cried out, doubling over, when Orion stabbed his stiff fingers into his midriff. When the reached for his gun, Orion jumped and kicked him in the chest with both legs, landing on top of him as they both toppled to the ground.

A waive of painful shocks hit Orion from different locations. It proved too much for him. He managed to neutralize most of the energy entering his body, but some of it paralyzed him temporarily.

He saw the group of guards approaching him and relaxed, fighting the paralysis while they carried him away. By the time they reached their destination, he had regained almost full control over his limbs again.

He opened his eyes when they dumped him unceremoniously on the hard ground and looked at the baldheaded man who loomed over him.

He found himself in a large, bright-lit room, the walls covered with vision-screens and other electronic equipment. How foolish they had been, to think they could walk around undetected. Surely, a place like this had all kinds of detection devices throughout the whole complex. However, living under primitive surroundings for a while sometimes made him careless when back in civilization with all its computers and machines.

"Well, well. It's you. What else can you do besides reading minds?"

"Reading minds?" Orion asked,

"Come, come," The tall man gave him an icy stare. "Don't play games with me. I know."

Since there was no reason to pretend, Orion rose to his feet. He was a big man himself, but he had to look up when he faced the other one.

"So you're the big wheel around here," he said coldly, anger and hate building up inside him. It would be easy and almost a pleasure to kill the slave trader, but it would also be foolish. He saw the guards, their weapons casually trained on him. They would surely kill him if he made a wrong move.

The slave trader gave him an evil smile. "My word is law here. All I have to do is snap my fingers and you're a dead man, slave!" His dark eyes bored into Orion's, who stared back at him, preparing himself for a mental attack.

But none came.

Suddenly, the black-clad man started to laugh. It sounded hollow and unholy. "You are not afraid of me, are you, slave? What is your name?"

"It is Orion. Hektor Orion. Maybe you should remember it."

The slave trader stopped laughing. "I just might," he said and waved his hand.

"Take him away!"

Chapter Twenty

The next day the slaves were loaded back aboard the interspace transporter. It would take them to the ship of the Insectoids.

Pressed close together in the cargo hold most of the slaves stared sullenly at each other. Nobody spoke. Except for the steady low hum of the ship's drive, only silence hung in the room.

Something began nagging at Orion's sub-consciousness and it finally hit him. Failing to see the cat-woman, he asked, "Did anyone see Sheenah?"

When the others shook their heads, he probed the ship for her pattern, but failed to detect anything.

"I don't think she's on board," he said, puzzled.

Lu-onna shrugged. "Maybe she's on a different ship."

"Or maybe she broke free," Val suggested.

"There's no place to go." Orion looked at Lu-onna. "We've come to the end of our journey it seems."

He turned when someone touched his arm and saw Ross, one of the twin-brothers beside him.

You must leave the ship now," Ross said to him.

Orion chucked. "We would if we could."

"You can," said his brother Trevor. "We know who and what you are."

"Really?" Orion gave the young man a sharp look. "What are we?"

"Carriers," Ross said with a low voice to prevent the other prisoners from hearing.

From deep inside Orion a warning rose up, his mind shifted his body into alert. "I don't know what you're talking about," he said.

Ross smiled. "We are not what we seem." His body wavered, the outlines of his face and head blurred, changed, and moments later Orion stared into the alien, multifaceted eyes of one of the insectoid races. Mandibles clicked around a small mouth. "We are not human, but we are not your enemies." The words sounded strange coming from the alien mouth.

Trevor's face had not changed. He held out his hand, displayed a ring identical to the Orion wore. "We are your contact," Trevor said.

"I don't understand."

"Some of our High Councils have been working with your governments. We want to stop the trading of human slaves, and we want to eliminate the common threat we are facing, the threat of the Dark Hunters."

"You are not like us," Orion stated.

Trevor grinned, looking almost boyish. "No," he said, "we are not. We are not carriers, but we have evolved, mutated. We can transform our bodies into the likeness of others. Even or minds."

Orion touched the other's mind, with astonishment. "You are not a telepath?"

"No, I'm not." Trevor shook his head. "I have other abilities." He pulled the ring from his finger, handed it to Orion. "Give this to Val. The rings have special properties, they will help you with melding your minds. You have to leave now. Go back to the moon. You will find assistance there."

Ross, who had changed back to his human form, nodded. "Trust us. We are not deceiving you. There is not much time."

"He is right," Lu-onna said, "we have to leave the ship now."

Zegg nodded. "I agree. Once we're in the Mothership of the Insectoids and we enter *Overspace*, there will be no way to escape, and once in *The Hive*, we'll never come back."

"I know." Orion hesitated, still secretly hoping to find Delina again, but he knew the others were right. "We'll try," he said, knowing they must succeed. He also knew the displacement of energy would betray their presence to any Dark Hunter in this region of space. A chance they had to take.

He looked at Val who gave him a brave smile. She trusted him. He could not disappoint her.

They sat on the floor in the lotus position, forming a circle, their naked bodies touching, hands linked.

The other prisoners watched them listlessly. Orion felt sorry for them, but he could not help them. Ross gave him an encouraging smile.

Orion's mind touched Lu-onna's, then Val's, and then Zegg's. They opened up, their life energies flowing into each other…joining…merging. They became one. He/they knew they couldn't transfer their physical bodies very far in space without damaging them. The closest place was the little moon they had come from. The shuttle they knew was there would take them back to Izzard-Junction.

I am afraid, came Val's impulses. *I have never done this before.*

Neither have I. Zegg sent. *Question? Lu-onna. Hektor…I perceive difference.* Awed. *Who…?*

Orion and Lu-onna joined them closer together.

You will know. No time to explain. Concentrate.

They entered High Mind. Reached out. .

The molecules of their physical bodies changed, moved through space, but something was still holding them back, interfered. Orion felt a sudden surge of power. It came from the ring on his finger. He sensed the power emanating from the rings of the others

They were close…closer…closer…Now!

Done.

Their minds separated, reluctantly. There was peace and serenity in the joining.

The space shuttle stood still in its place. Everything seemed quiet inside the building where they had materialized.

"Let's hurry," Orion said. "There are guards around. I sense them."

The teleportation of their bodies had weakened him, drained his life energies. The others were weak, too, but he had been the driving force. Lu-onna swayed beside him. He steadied her, put an arm around her naked shoulders, feeling her shiver.

"Are you alright?" he asked. She nodded, smiling weakly. She had given much of herself, to protect Val, who was still a fledgling, untrained. And Zegg, not of their kind. His alien mind had dragged them back, but they could not have left him behind, he was their brother. His race was evolving fast, almost faster then the human race and it would reach the next level sooner than expected.

They never reached the entrance to the shuttle. The dark presence of the Hunter hit like a bolt of lightening.

Orion swung around, instinctively spinning a protective cocoon around himself and his companions. Lu-onna's web of pure energy melded with his. They had no more reason to hide the Power. The Dark Hunter had revealed himself. He knew who and what they were.

Orion cursed himself. He should have guessed the instant he saw the slave trader. He couldn't have known for sure, because a Dark Hunter could not be recognized unless he chose to reveal himself. Since the Hunters were shape shifters they could assume any form they chose, but they liked to show off their diabolical powers.

"So the Hunt finally ends." He was still in his human form, but he had cast off all his mental barriers. He spoke verbally, not being able to use mind-speech. A long red cape hung loose from his wide shoulders, his eyes glowed dark in his white face, his shaven skull gleamed dully in the bright lights.

He pointed a long finger at the little group, smiling sardonically.

"Very impressive," Orion said, "but let's stop playing childish games."

The Dark Hunter's laughter echoed deep and hollow from the metal walls of the hangar. "You don't like playing games?" he thundered. "You and your kind have been playing with us far too long. You thought you were gods until we taught you otherwise. No, we don't play games anymore. There is no escape from the energy field we created around this station."

His human form dissolved while he spoke, changed shape. The head became narrow, triangular, the body long and sinuous until he no longer looked human. Before them writhed the ancient enemy…The Serpent.

"Now I'll show you who your true master is," the Serpent hissed and launched himself at Orion, changing in midair to an arrow of light.

The Hunter struck, colliding with the energy shield Orion had created with the help of Lu-onna. A blinding explosion and an ear-deafening crash shook the floor, the walls and the ceiling of the hangar as the two forces clashed.

The humans were thrown against the shuttle from the terrible force and the long body of the Hunter, solid again, crashed to the ground. He lay unmoving for an instant, and then he slithered back, his triangular head close to the floor.

"You're stronger than expected," the Serpent hissed, rolling his body into a tight coil and then, without warning, he struck again.

And again and again.

Orion felt his powers weakening. Lu-onna lay by his side, her body still, all of her energy feeding the mind-shield, but he sensed her life force ebbing away. The Hunter was strong, much too strong. Orion knew they might lose.

Sorrow welled up inside him, sorrow for Val and Zegg and all the others like them. The Serpents would hunt them down. They would never allow them to evolve any further. Once they'd destroyed the last of the *Chosen*, there would be nothing to hold the Hunters back.

Suddenly he sensed something was wrong. He felt Val's presence behind him, but not Zegg's. The reptilian was gone. He had slipped out of the protective web.

Why? Where had he gone?

He sensed something else. The energy screen protecting the station had disappeared.

The Hunter must have sensed it too. He stopped his furious attacks and lay hissing on the ground, his great triangular head swaying back and forth. "Where is the *Scaly One*?" he hissed and then he roared angrily. "The screen is gone! The little primitive must have found the generating unit!"

Orion felt Lu-onna stirring beside him. She had used the short moment of rest to build new strength, feeding from the primal life energies all around them.

The Hunter became aware of it and, hissing, he attacked again, his energy body crashing into their stronger shield, determined not to let them strengthen it more.

We can't hold out much longer. Lu-onna's weak pulsing thought reached Orion. There had not been enough time for her to regenerate her life force. Orion felt his own weakening, and he was much stronger than she had ever been. Stronger than any of the others and yet…even his own power would not be enough.

Something touched his mind, a shy, uncertain life force, but strong, very strong.

Can I help?

Val!

He engulfed her, carefully let her energy blend with his and Lu-onna's. She was not trained in this kind of combat, not trained in any kind of violence.

Her powers were an unknown factor and she must be protected. She learned, fast, controlling the *Power* now. The shield strengthened, held.

The Hunter hissed and screamed furiously, his eyes blazing like miniature suns.

Two figures rushed toward him from the side.

Orion recognized Zegg and Sheenah. They held lasers in their hands.

The Hunter saw them too, turned his attention toward them. Zegg pointed his weapon at the Serpent, releasing the trigger.

Orion sensed the bundle of raw energy speeding toward the Dark Hunter, who in an instant's flash changed into a creature of energy and absorbed the deadly ray, leaving him unharmed.

Only in his physical form would he have been fatally wounded.

A lightening bolt shot from him, aimed at the reptilian, but the killing stroke never reached the target. Suddenly, there was a protective force field between Zegg and the Hunter and the bolt hit with a deafening clang.

"I've been tricked," screamed the Hunter. "Tricked by a mere mortal." He slithered toward the rear of the hangar, unable to hold the energy form much longer.

There was another *Presence* now in the hangar, he joined his powers with them and together they prevented the Hunter from changing into the energy level. Sheenah and Zegg took advantage of the Serpent's weakness and sprayed the writhing body with their laser beams.

The body of the Dark Hunter disintegrated and was gone.

They all turned and looked at their ally who had so suddenly come to their aid.

The newcomer gave the *High Sign of the Ancients.* Only Orion and Lu-onna understood the high-level impulses.

I am honored to have been of assistance to you, High Lord, he said in mind speech, addressing Orion.

Thank you, my brother. Orion's thoughts welcomed the other one, knowing he was talking to a *Carrier of the Ancient Memory,* not at all surprised to see a member of the Insectoids. The surviving Ancients had spread themselves all over the Galaxy, entering the minds of the many different species they encountered.

Carefully, they'd guided and taught the brutes, some of them not much more than animals, improving the genes by spreading their seeds, impregnating as many females as possible. Slowly they led the primitive intelligences out of the dark ages. It hat taken thousands of years, some falling back through catastrophes, natural or artificially caused by the Dark Hunters who were determined not to let these races evolve to the next level.

Now they finally were almost ready. Many of the Dark Hunters had been destroyed, but also many of the *Chosen Carriers* in this war that lasted endless millennia.

The last of the Ancients died a long time ago, but they lived on in the Chosen, each one of them carrying within him or her the essence of one of the Ancients, like Orion, like Lu-onna, and like their new ally. He had no name, but Orion would recognize him by his mind pattern if they should ever meet again.

We will stop the taking of human slaves, came the impulses of the Insectoid and Orion nodded, his thoughts linking again with the other mind.

There is one I have been searching for, he questioned, sending the memory pattern of Delina.

Impulses of sad sympathy came from the Insectoid. *I don't*

*know if I can be of much help, High Lord, but I will try to find
your lost mind-sister. If I do, I will make arrangements to send
her home.*

His mind closed abruptly. Stiffly, he turned and walked
toward the airlock. Orion looked after him, smiling, and then his
gaze fell on the cat-woman who was staring at him with large
luminous eyes.

She grinned, coming closer, the laser dangling in her hands.
"I knew there was something peculiar about you," she said, "but
what it is I can hardly guess. I still don't know what exactly
happened here. It certainly was mighty exciting. Maybe I should
stick around. You seem to lead an interesting life."

She stood close to him, searching his face. "What are you,
Hektor Orion?"

He shrugged. "A man…as you should know."

Touching his face, she shook her head. "You know what I
mean. From the outside you look humanoid, but are you?"

Again, she surprised him with her powers of intuition.
"Would it make a difference?" he asked softly.

"No," she said. "I would have loved you anyway." She
brushed his lips with a quick kiss and stepped back.

He noticed the moisture in her eyes and reached for her. "I am
glad you are alive," he said, taking her into his arms. For a
moment, she nestled against him, and then she pushed him away.
"Let's get off this rock and back to civilization."

Epilogue

They sat in the inn. Orion, Lu-onna, and Val. Sheenah had already left with Zegg. The reptilian had convinced the cat-woman to come with him, promising her an exciting life as a foreign agent.

Orion smiled ruefully when he thought of her last words before she boarded the space liner. "Too bad you are so different, big man. You and I…we would have fit together." Winking, she added, "In many ways."

This was best. He could not have tied her to him. He had a job to do, while she only sought adventure. *Like most of these people,* he thought, looking over the crowd in the inn.

Drifters, adventurers, and a few criminals, either hiding from persecution or looking for a mark. It made no difference. On Izzard-Junction, they were safe either way.

He had his mind-shield up. No sense to leave himself open to so many chattering minds. He turned in surprise when he heard a familiar rasping voice behind him.

"I didn't think they'd keep you long." A large hand clasped his shoulder. "I am glad to see you free."

Orion looked at the guide's smiling face.

"Why?" he asked coldly.

"I told you I liked you." Giles tipped his wide-brimmed hat. "Well, maybe we'll run into each other again."

Watching the short man's wide back, Orion shook his head.

"He sure has nerves, that bastard," Lu-onna said. "What made him think we wouldn't kill him on sight?"

Orion shrugged, chuckling. "Like you said, he has nerves." He waved his hand. "Look around you. If you want to bring justice to this place, you might as well kill half these people in here."

"Why did you let him get away?" Val asked, not understanding.

He took her hand into his. His mind opened to her, sensing the excitement and fear she experienced.

You have a lot to learn, little sister. The whole universe is a jungle. We can only try to change it a little at a time and let evolution run its course.

The End

For a list of Herbert's other books visit his website at:

http://www.hegro.blogspot.com/

www.ingramcontent.com/pod-product-compliance
Lightning Source LLC
Chambersburg PA
CBHW030337180626
46810CB00003B/1389